Jackie French's writing career spans 12 years, 36 wombats, 102 books for kids and adults, nine languages, various awards, assorted 'Burke's Backyard' segments in a variety of disguises, radio shows, newspaper and magazine columns, theories of pest and weed ecology and 28 shredded back doormats. The doormats are the victims of the wombats, who require constant appeasement in the form of carrots, rolled oats and wombat nuts, which is one of the reasons for her prolific output: it pays the carrot bills.

Her most recent awards include the 2000 Children's book Council Book of the Year Award for Younger Readers for *Hitler's Daughter*, which also won the 2002 U.K. Wow! Award for the most inspiring children's Book of the year, and the 2002 Aurealis Award for Younger Readers for *Café on Callisto*.

For more on Jackie French, her wombats and her books, zap onto her website: www.jackiefrench.com or subscribe to her free monthly newsletter about her books and wombats at: www.harpercollins.com.au/jackiefrench

D1150495

# VALLEY
## *of* GOLD

### JACKIE FRENCH

![Angus&Robertson logo] Angus&Robertson
An imprint of HarperCollins*Publishers*

**Angus&Robertson**
An imprint of HarperCollins*Publishers*

First published in Australia in 2003
Reprinted in 2003 (three times)
by HarperCollins*Publishers* Pty Limited
ABN 36 009 913 517
A member of the HarperCollins*Publishers* (Australia) Pty Limited Group
www.harpercollins.com.au

**HarperCollins*Publishers***
25 Ryde Road, Pymble, Sydney NSW 2073, Australia
31 View Road, Glenfield, Auckland 10, New Zealand
77–85 Fulham Palace Road, London W6 8JB, United Kingdom
Hazelton Lanes, 55 Avenue Road, Suite 2900, Toronto, Ontario, M5R 3L2
*and* 1995 Markham Road, Scarborough, Ontario, M1B 5M8, Canada
10 East 53rd Street, New York NY 10022, USA

National Library of Australia Cataloguing-in-publication data:

French, Jackie.
    For primary school age children.
    ISBN 0 207 19988 4.
    I. Araluen region (N.S.W.) – History – Juvenile fiction.
    I.Title.
A823.3

Cover Images:   gold pan from photolibrary.com; children from
                John Oxley Library, neg. no. 33600
Designed by Lore Foye, HarperCollins Design Studio
Printed and bound in Australia by Griffin Press on 80gsm Econoprint

8  7  6  5  4      03  04  05  06

# CONTENTS

| | |
|---|---|
| Author's Note | vii |
| Four billion years BCE: The birth of gold | 1 |
| 35,000 BCE: The last of the tigers | 4 |
| 40,000 BCE – 1850 ACE | 11 |
| 1853: Gold! | 15 |
| 1853 – 1860 | 29 |
| 1863: The golden walls | 31 |
| 1860 – 1870 | 55 |
| 1865: The night of the bushranger | 58 |
| 1870 – 1890 | 76 |
| 1900: Maggie | 78 |
| 1890 – 1920 | 85 |
| 1922: Alice and the Yowie | 88 |
| 1920 – 1972 | 114 |
| 1972: True gold | 118 |
| 1972 – 2002 | 156 |
| 2002: A true story | 162 |
| 2003 | 167 |

# Author's Note

This book is not the history of the Araluen Valley, because I live here, and if my neighbours recognised themselves or their ancestors, they might throw stones at my windows. (No, they wouldn't; they're nice, but I'm not going to risk it.) Also, if I say this book is imaginary, no one can say: 'Hey, that didn't happen till 1853.'

None of the stories in this book ever happened, and certainly no one in them is based on any real person, but they *might* have happened. Sometimes stories can give you more of an idea of how people thought and lived than pages from a history book can.

On the other hand, this book was inspired by the history of the Araluen Valley: all its history, from the moment the planet earth — and what was to become the valley and its gold — condensed out of a star four and a half billion years ago, until today, when I wrote the last sentence of this book.

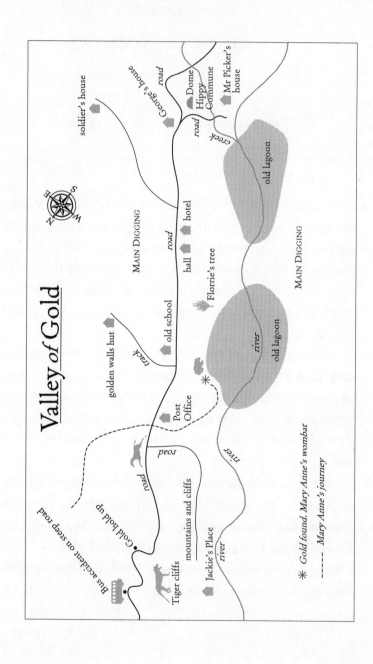

# Valley of Gold

soldier's house

George's house

road

road

Dome
Hippy
Commune

Mr Picker's
house

MAIN DIGGING

road

hotel

old lagoon

creek

golden walls hut

old school

hall

Florrie's tree

track

MAIN DIGGING

old lagoon

river

Post
Office

road

road

mountains and cliffs

river

Gold hold up

Bus accident on steep road

Jackie's Place

river

Tiger cliffs

\* *Gold found. Mary Anne's wombat*

----- *Mary Anne's journey*

# The Birth of the Gold

The gold was born in an ancient sun then spun flaming into the darkness to become part of the heart of the planet earth four billion years ago.

The new planet cooled into land and sea. Two supercontinents formed and broke then formed again into the third giant continent, the Antarctic land of Gondwana.

This is where the valley began eighty million years ago. Volcanoes thundered across Gondwana. Deep in the heart of the earth the molten rock that held the gold was forced up to spread across the land.

The valley formed slowly. The land slipped and folded and the mountain ranges rose (they're still rising now). The rain that fell on the ranges became streams that joined to make a river that began to cut the valley out from the rock and soil.

Forty-five million years ago the land that would become Australia (including the young river valley) slipped away from the Antarctic. By now the great age of dinosaurs had come and gone; they had died out, killed by the climate change and by earth's collision with a giant meteor that crashed half a world away.

In those days the valley was far from the sea. Slowly the eastern edges of Australia sank into the ocean and disappeared.

The valley grew deeper as the river flooded through it, and the mountains around it grew still higher. There were flowers in the valley now and conifers, cycads and ferns, and it was watered by warm soft rain. The world outside grew colder and drier. Grassland and deserts spread, but the valley sheltered its trees.

And the gold? The rocks thrown out by the volcanoes were weathered into soil and gravel. The floods that washed through the valley carried the soil with them. But the gold was heavier than the soil. It dropped into bends in the creeks and river. It sparkled in sandy crevices or lay deep below new layers of sand and soil.

In other parts of the world volcanoes still spat out new soil with their magma, and glaciers carried soil and left it behind when they melted. But here in Australia the soil was already old, except in places like the valley, where the river flooded and left leaves, logs, animals droppings or ground-up rocks that replenished the soil and kept it fertile.

It was a rich valley. Herds of massive, flat-faced roos grazed on the hills; giant birds, emu-sized and larger, strode through the forest; echidnas the size of dogs dug for termites in the fallen logs; wombat-like monsters tore down branches and chewed the leaves.

The animals changed the land. Their dung spread the seeds of plants they liked to eat. They pruned the young shrubs as they ate them so they grew bushy. They helped to keep it fertile so that other plants could grow by returning the plants they ate to the soil.

All animals change the land just as the land changes them. But humans change the land most of all.

And forty thousand years ago, humans came to the valley.

## 35,000 BCE

# THE LAST OF THE TIGERS

They called them the Tiger Cliffs, though it had been years since anyone had hunted a tiger there. But sometimes at night, as the campfire sank down to dark red coals, the last of the daisy yams eaten and the meat picked off the bones of yesterday's roast kangaroo, a howl drifted down from the pale grey rocks above the valley and the families wondered if the strange howl was a tiger's.

No other tiger's call ever answered the howl from the cliffs. If there was still a tiger up there, it was the last.

No one had seen a tiger for years. But there were stories of an ancient hunter who'd cast a fresh tiger skin down in front of his beloved, and she'd worn it all the years of her life — the only woman in the camp to wear a tiger skin.

Mirrigan sometimes wondered if that hunter had also felt that he was different, had felt the need to do one great, incredible thing so everyone else would know that he was different too.

I'll find the tiger today, thought Mirrigan. I'll throw its skin on the ground by Dhani, and when she sees it ... He wasn't quite sure what Dhani would do when she saw the tiger skin, but she'd know that he was brave and ... and ...

Mirrigan hoisted his spears over to his other shoulder. The valley narrowed here, the river frothing steep and wild between the cliffs. Further down it spread out into deep lagoons, filled with ducks and fish and eels.

Anyone could catch a fish or grab a duck by swimming quietly beneath it and pulling its feet under the water. But to spear a tiger!

Mirrigan began to climb. Soft soil and grasses gave way to tussocks. Thin trees grasped rocks and clay. High above an eagle peered down at him. It circled twice then glided slowly down into the valley, as though to say, 'You won't do anything of interest here'.

Mirrigan kept on climbing.

Now the cliffs began, sheer rock faces and piles of boulders that sat for years till rain or animals dislodged them, sending them bouncing down the mountain to brake into jagged chunks beside the river.

Mirrigan bent down and sniffed.

He could smell wombat, and those hairs were from a brush-tailed wallaby (too tough to make good eating) and those droppings were a possum's. If he looked up, he'd see possum scratches on the trees.

Possum skin was soft, but he wasn't after possums.

Yes, there was another smell, not just possum and wombat. Meat-eaters smelt different. Spotted quolls' droppings smelt of what they ate, and so did human leavings ... Tigers' droppings would smell of dead meat.

So there was a tiger up here! But how would he find it?

Mirrigan gazed around. The tiger could be anywhere up here, among the rocks. But even tigers had to drink, and the river was a long way down. Besides, the tiger would drink in a different place every night, where it might catch unwary wombats or a wallaby.

Where could a tiger drink up here?

Mirrigan studied the green folds of the mountains. Yes, there was a gully over there, a dark fold between the hills. Dark trees meant damp soil and maybe pools of water between the rocks. He edged towards it, walking softly in the way he'd learnt when he was small, pressing the sides of his feet into the rocky ground so that not even a guard kangaroo, listening for danger while the rest of the herd ate, could hear his footsteps.

Something lay between two boulders. A dead wallaby. He poked it with his spear. Only the head was left, cracked and jagged bones, and the long teeth grinning up at him, but he could see it had been a young one, not one that had died of old age. A wallaby was too big for a quoll to kill, and goannas preferred to eat the leftovers from other animals' kills.

Only two things could have killed the wallaby.

Humans — or a tiger.

Mirrigan could smell the damp soil of the gully now, the rotting leaves, the ferns, the scents of all the animals that had drunk here the night before. And yes, there *was* a pool, a thin gleam of water seeping over an edge of rock, and there were wombat droppings and wallaby pellets and ... and something else.

He knelt down and examined it.

It was an animal dropping. He'd never seen one like it before, long and dark and filled with hairs. It could almost have been an eagle's dropping. But it wasn't.

Tiger. It had to be a tiger's.

The dropping was fresh. The tiger must be near here, it would come again at dusk to drink.

Mirrigan gazed around the gully. Where should he hide? Up a tree would be best, one of the smooth-barked myrtle trees, but he'd have to hope the tiger approached from the other side of the gully or it would smell where he'd been and stay away ...

Something growled behind him.

Mirrigan froze. It took all the control he possessed not to swing around to see what was behind him. A sudden move might make the animal attack. A sudden move would be death.

Slowly, slowly, slowly he turned.

The tiger watched him, black and gold in the shadows.

It must have smelt him, he thought dazedly. It must have hunted him, just as he hunted the tiger. Of course, he thought, the tiger eats meat just as I eat meat, and I am meat too.

Mirrigan had hunted since he was small. For the first time in his life he realised what it was like to be prey. It had never occurred to him that *he* might die up here, not the tiger. But now it did.

The tiger was smaller than he'd thought it would be, not even as high as his waist. Its head looked too small for its body. But the shoulders were wide and muscular and the jaws strong enough to crush his bones, just like it had cracked the bones of the wallaby to suck out the marrow.

The tiger crouched. The bulky shoulders rippled. Suddenly there was no time to think, only time to grab his spear as the tiger leapt. The massive chest crashed into the spear point, knocking the wide jaws sideways so they didn't reach his throat.

Blood wept onto the yellow fur around the spear. The tiger staggered to its feet, the spear protruding from its chest. It grunted deep in its throat. Ignoring the spear in its chest, it leapt again.

For a moment its jaws grasped his arm. Mirrigan felt teeth and pain. But somehow he managed to grasp the spear with his other hand and twist and push it further in.

Then suddenly it was over. The agony in his arm lessened as the jaws let go. The tiger leant against him for one long moment, then fell. Its body lay black and gold among the ferns. The blood stopped flowing round the spear shaft.

Mirrigan's arm was bleeding too, but it didn't matter. It would heal.

Mirrigan knelt at the spring and washed the wound clean, then drank. For a moment he felt giddy as his blood washed into the water, but it passed.

The tiger was still lying there. It looked even smaller now, in death. The gold of its coat seemed

duller. The last tiger, he thought. I have killed the last tiger in the valley. Me!

Slowly he pulled at the spear again till it came out. He used its sharp blade to slit the tiger's fur and pull away the guts. It took longer to punch the skin away from the flesh. His arm ached even more. His blood joined the tiger's on its skin.

But it didn't matter. He'd killed the tiger.

It was almost dark now, but he could see by starlight and soon there'd be a moon. Down in the valley a camp fire glowed. Mirrigan imagined himself walking into the firelight, the bloody tiger skin around his shoulders.

It was only as he climbed down the cliffs more carefully now — as his arm screamed with pain and, despite the moonlight, he had to be careful where he put his feet — he realised that he'd never hear the tiger's call again.

What had the tiger called for? he wondered suddenly. Had it hoped, year after year, that one night another tiger would answer? What had it felt like to be the last of your kind, alone? And suddenly he felt empty, as though some part of him had vanished with the tiger.

The tiger skin stank even after the skin had dried, and the fur was coarse, but Dhani wore it just the same, and people talked about the tiger hunt for many years.

But no one heard a tiger's howl again. They don't even call them Tiger Cliffs any more. They're just the cliffs where Mirrigan speared the tiger. And one day even that memory will be gone.

# 40,000 BCE – 1850 ACE

Humans first came to the valley from the north travelling up the river from the coast, hunting for game as they went.

The valley must have seemed a paradise. Ducks flew about the wide river; fish swam below the water lilies in the lagoon. Bright yellow flowers grew all along the valley floor and the hills were rich in game like palorchestes — a giant clawed animal a bit like a furry, long-nosed bull — and wabula, a small kangaroo-like animal that's extinct now too.

The smaller animals were hunted by marsupial lions and the tiger that Mirrigan hunted, which wasn't the Tasmanian tiger (*Thylacinus cynocephalus*), but the bigger 'powerful tiger' (*Thylacinus potens*).

These giant animals disappeared from the valley a few thousand years after humans arrived. Humans had hunted them, but the land was also slowly drying up as the world grew colder, and moisture was locked up in snow and glaciers.

The river in the valley shrank; its swamps and billabongs dried up, and the shrubs the giant animals fed on died in the cold and drought. Even if humans had never come to the valley, the giant animals would probably have died out.

But humans had made the valley even drier. They brought 'firestick' farming: they burnt the tablelands above the valley so that lush grass would grow when the rain fell on the burnt land. Mobs of kangaroos would come to feed on the new grass and provide easy meat for the human hunters.

Slowly the mixed forest on the tablelands changed to gum trees and grasslands that would grow again after the fires, and these trees made the fires even fiercer, as the oils in gum trees burn hot and fast. Lusher trees grew only in the valley now, in the gullies that were too damp to burn.

The new gum trees dropped fewer leaves, and the fires burnt the dead grass that might otherwise have rotted back into the soil. The tableland soil no longer held as much moisture as it had before, and the water that had seeped down to the valley slowly grew less and less. The river shrank to a wide creek and billabongs.

But most of the valley was too wet to burn and too steep for mobs of roos except on the lower hills. The valley was a place where you could feast on other things. There were ducks to catch in the shallows (you swam under them quietly and dragged them down by the feet, then roasted them on the fire). There were echidnas to roast too (the fire singed off their bristles) and honey from the small dark bees that didn't sting, so if you followed a bee back to its nest in the hollow branch, you could chop it down and scoop out thick rich honeycomb.

But best of all were the endless daisy yams with their thick, sweet roots to bake by the fire, and the waterlilies that grew in the broad lagoons. You could roast the waterlily seeds or grind them to make flat cakes that you baked on hot rocks. You could eat the tubers baked, or dried and ground into flour for more cakes.

The family groups met in peace in the valley, to feast and to dance and to renew the ceremonies of ownership and duty to the land.

Then fifteen thousand years ago the world grew cold again, and the gentle life in the valley changed. The trees died; the lagoons dried up to a thin winding creek. The humans moved back to the warmer coastlands, where at least the sea still gave them fish and shellfish. Grass covered the valley now, and there were twisted snow gums on the ridges.

But a few red gums and casuarinas and other trees survived in the sheltered gullies. When the ice finally melted trees colonised the valley again. Ducks flew back to the lagoons, and once more the families feasted.

In those days change came slowly over thousands of years. Then in 1821 new humans came to the valley. They had sailed from an alien land across the world, where life was different. These settlers came from lands with young fertile soils, where it rained every few days.

To many of them, Australia was a terrifying place: a wilderness without the fences and canals and roads of the lands they'd known. (To the Aboriginal inhabitants, of course, it wasn't a wilderness at all, but a land where they knew each rock and which tree yielded the best wild cherries.)

Like the first humans to come here, the new settlers came to the valley up the river from the coast. Now the valley changed again, as it had changed with all new inhabitants.

The settlers chopped down trees to make room to plant their wheat and corn and potatoes. They planted new trees — plums and quinces and pears and persimmons. The new settlers grew to love the valley, but they didn't understand it. They didn't realise how cutting down trees led to salt rising up through the soil, till nothing could grow in the salty desert; how the wheat they grew destroyed the soil; how the feet of their animals made the land so hard that rain couldn't soak deep into the ground.

The forest changed too. There were still tall trees and leafy shadows, but now the land under the trees was clear, as the cattle's heavy feet compacted the ground so that young shrubs couldn't break through and those that did were eaten by the strange new animals. The yam daisies vanished. In dry times the cattle waded in the lagoons so their edges turned into swamps.

The valley was large, and there were still few settlers. But the next change was to be more drastic than any the valley had ever known since the time of the volcanoes.

# 1853

# GOLD!

The vampire* flew over her just as the moonlight began to thread through the trees. Mary Anne screamed and pulled the blanket over her face.

'Mary, love, what is it?'

'Up in the tree! A vampire!'

The big man sat up. He pushed the hair out of his eyes and tried to smile, but worry had bitten deep into his face. 'Sure, love, there are no vampires here. Your Uncle James would have writ us if there'd been vampires.'

Mary Anne peered out from under the blanket. 'But there was! I saw it! It — aah! There it is! Shoot it, Papa, before it sucks our blood!'

Her father peered up into the trees just as the vampire launched itself off another branch and glided down to the next tree. He shook his head. 'That's no vampire, love.'

'But it flies! And it looked down at me and ...'

'Birds fly, darling. And vampires don't have furry

---

* Mary Anne's vampire was a greater glider. They like blossom, not blood!

faces, do they? It's some sort of possum, I reckon. A possum that flies, or glides, more like. Shh, you settle down now. There's nothing out there that can harm you.'

Her father pushed his blanket off and poked at the fire so the sparks shot up into the night, then threw on more dead branches. The trees in this strange land were always dropping branches, thought Mary Anne, as though they didn't want them any more. But at least it made it easy to collect wood for the fire.

'See?' said her father. 'A nice bright fire to keep the vampires away. Can you sleep now?'

'No,' said Mary Anne honestly.

'How about I tell you a story then?' Her father lowered himself down onto the ground beside her. 'A story about a ... a princess and her father, hey? Heading to a new land? They travelled by coach and they travelled by ship, oh, many months across the water, then they landed at Sydney Town and bought their horses and their stores and headed out to make their fortune in the bush ...'

His words floated over her. Mary Anne gazed up at the moon, floating big and yellow between the white branches of the tree. Branches shouldn't be white, thought Mary Anne. They're like ghost trees. Behind her the horses shuffled in their hobbles as they tore at the tussocks of grass. At least that was a comforting sound. A normal sound. Not a horrible strange sound from this horrible strange country ...

'And soon her father had made enough money for a farm of their own. A magic farm it was, with cows as fat as barrels and the princess grew fat as butter. And they all lived happily ever after.' Her father smiled at her. 'What do you think of that then?'

But it hadn't happened like that, thought Mary Anne. That story had nothing about Mama dying of fever on the ship or the grubs in the ship's biscuit or the drunks that yelled at them in Sydney Town. It didn't have the flies or the brown snakes that lay in wait to bite you or furry vampires gliding through the trees.

And if the beginning of the story wasn't true, maybe the end wasn't either. Maybe Papa would never make enough money to buy a farm, working for Uncle James in this valley place they were going to. And, even if they did have a farm, it would just be a shack, like the bark-roofed huts they had seen on their way here, not a proper house at all. Even Uncle James's house had a dirt floor and no glass in the windows. And there would be flies, thought Mary Anne sleepily, the clouds of flies that gathered in your nose and eyes ...

'Sleep now,' said Papa. He settled back in his blanket, his head pillowed on his saddle. 'We should see the valley tomorrow. It's a grand place, James says.'

Soon he was snoring.

Mary Anne shut her eyes and thought of home. Green fields and proper houses and ducks on the pond ... She was nearly asleep when she felt hot breath over her face.

'Papa?' she asked sleepily.

Red eyes stared down at her. Red eyes and white teeth and ...

'Papa!'

The beast growled at her. It was a dog, a wild dog, a warrigal or dingo*. And there were more of them — three, four ... no, more.

'Papa!'

The dingo took a step back, growling. Another second, thought Mary Anne, and it will leap at my throat. She twisted and grabbed the saddlecloth behind her and flicked it at the dingo. One edge of it caught the animal's nose. It stepped back further, its eyes watchful. Somewhere another dingo snarled.

What was it doing? Was it eating Papa? Then she'd be alone in this horrible bush and ...

Fire! Mrs Hanrahan on the boat said that dingoes were afraid of fire. She scrambled up and grabbed one of the branches from the fire and waved the burning end of it high above her head, so sparks flared out around the camp.

'Shoo!' she screamed. 'Shoo!'

It seemed a silly thing to say, like scaring a kitten from the cream back home. But either her words or the sparks must have scared the dogs; they backed away, and now Papa was there too, a flaming branch in his hand as well.

'Get on with you!' he thundered. 'Back now! Back!'

The dingoes retreated into the darkness. But not far, thought Mary Anne. They were still there among the trees, watching.

* The dingoes were probably after the leftovers from Mary Anne and her father's dinner.

Papa piled more wood on the fire. The flames shot up. The red light pushed the darkness back. But not far enough, thought Mary Anne. Not nearly far enough.

'Bring your blanket closer to the fire,' said Papa hoarsely. 'I'll stand watch and keep the fire piled up. They won't come close while it's burning high.'

Mary Anne nodded. She didn't ask what would have happened if they'd both been asleep when the dingoes came. There had been a piece in the paper about dingoes the first day they'd landed at Sydney Town. The dingoes ate the heart out of you, the paper said, and your entrails too.

The fire crackled as she lay down beside it. She could feel its heat on her face, hear Papa's breathing and a whinny from Bobby. He must be frightened of the dingoes too.

Finally she slept.

Fog misted through the trees when she woke. White fog and white trees and long drops of water on the blue-green leaves that sparkled like diamonds as the sun shone through the mist. If only they really were diamonds, thought Mary Anne, we could buy our farm now. If only the sunlight were gold, we could slice a slab of it like butter and take it to the bank.

'Billy's boiling,' said Papa cheerfully. Too cheerfully, thought Mary Anne. Why did adults always speak to you like that, pretending everything was wonderful?

Mary Anne drank her tea, hot and thick with sugar, but no milk. She hadn't tasted milk since they'd left Sydney Town. Papa had made damper in the ashes too. It was heavy as a rock and tasted like one too, even with treacle on it. But she ate it anyway.

'When we have our kitchen,' said Papa, 'there'll be a big iron stove and you'll make bread as light as ever your mama did.' He stopped suddenly. It still hurt too much for both of them to think about Mama.

Papa saddled the horses, his big Mr Jones and Mary Anne's Bobby, and piled the packs on Sammy. 'Not far now,' he said encouragingly, though Mary Anne wondered if he were encouraging her or himself. 'We should reach the valley today and then it's only another day's ride down to James's.'

'Why isn't there a road, Papa?'

'I've told you, darling. There are only three farms in the whole valley. Who would build a road to it? But the track's clear enough, just as James writ me back home. See the marks on the trees? And there's been cattle this way too — see the droppings?'

Mary Anne nodded. It still seemed — impossible — that was the word — impossible, to head out through the trees where there was no road at all and expect to find a farm at the end of it.

It had been over a year since Papa had had a letter from Uncle James. Maybe a snake had bitten him. Maybe he was no longer even in the valley. Maybe they'd walk forever through the trees till the dingoes ate them or the vampire sucked their blood.

The fog lifted as the sun rose higher. Above it the sky blazed blue. Sky had no right to be as blue as that, thought Mary Anne. It needed clouds and softness and the trees should be a proper deep green with their bark on them neatly, not peeling away in crisp strips onto the ground.

The soil changed. They were heading downhill now. Bobby's hooves struck sharply against the shale. Quartz gleamed between the tussocks. Then suddenly, through the trees, she saw the valley.

It was deep and green, and water glinted gold and silver, and suddenly she could smell flowers. There was even a rainbow arching from one ridge to another. It all looked so much like a picture on a calender that Mary Anne laughed, and Papa grinned at her, relieved to see her happy.

'Who owns it, Papa?' she whispered.

'The valley? No one yet. It's all wild country, except for the three farms. Queen Victoria owns the rest, I suppose.'

'Does she run sheep here? The grass looks so short!'

'Ah, that'd be the kangaroos. No, darling. One day a bit of it will be ours. We'll tame it into a proper farm, just you see.'

'What about the black people? Do they own any of it?'

Papa laughed. 'What a thought! Come on, love. Not far to go now.'

Mary Anne felt her smile evaporate. Not long till what? Another horrible shanty with flies and hard work?

It was steep down the ridge — so steep in places that they had to dismount and lead the horses step by step. It seemed to take forever. The sun had sunk behind the ridge when they finally stopped, though Mary Anne thought it must only be late afternoon.

But it was beautiful. Even she had to admit that. The coarse tussocks of the tableland above had given way to fuzzy grass, so short it looked like the mowers had been here already, sweeping with their scythes. And all through the grass were flowers, more flowers than she'd ever seen, yellow daisies that turned their faces to the sun, and tiny pinks that winked among the green, and funny, fat, green flowers like tiny balloons. Tall ferns with trunks like trees were scattered among the forest, and there were even proper-looking trees, all round and dark with waxy blooms. Even the horrible gum trees were festooned with flowers, tiny white ones and tiny cream and purple trumpets and other trees had tiny buds of yellow.

Bobby snorted and jerked his head. 'He can smell the water,' said Papa. 'Come on, it's just through here.'

It was a broad lake, with a river flowing into it and trickling out the other end. There were even flowers on the water, waterlilies like on the village pond at home, but these were big and white. The lake was edged with sand like yellow lace around a tablecloth, and birds sang deep in among the trees.

'Not bad,' said Papa grinning. 'What do you say, darling? Not bad.'

Mary Anne nodded. It seemed disloyal to *say* it was beautiful: the most beautiful place she'd ever seen. Not without Mama to see it too. And besides, there were still the dingoes and vampires and giant poisonous snakes.

They made camp on the soft grass by the water. It seemed cruel to crush so many flowers with their blankets.

'No need for a fire yet,' said Papa. He looked down the long stretch of lake, turning and twisting between the long-armed trees. 'You stay here, girl and have a nap. It was precious little sleep you got last night. I'll take the musket and see if I can get a duck for dinner. Better than salt mutton, eh? You'll be alright here by yourself, just for a while.'

'Yes, Papa,' said Mary Anne because, after all, there was nothing else to say and he'd had less sleep even than her. Because you couldn't cry, 'Don't leave me all alone,' or even 'Take me home!' because there was no home now, not till Papa made enough money to build them one.

It was quiet in the clearing. Mary Anne leant against a tree. It had pale yellow bark, not like the grey-white bark of the trees above the valley, and the branches were long and stretched up towards the sky.

Mary Anne shut her eyes. If she slept sitting up, surely nothing bad could happen to her. The wild dogs and snakes and vampires would think she was awake.

It was a strange sleep. It was almost as though she wasn't asleep at all, as if she'd floated on the smell of flowers and water into another world, one that was almost this one, but so much better.

There was a waterhole, like this one, and gum trees too. But there were other trees now: familiar apple trees and pear trees and quinces and mulberries, and wooden fences around fields that were green, not brown, and fat cows with big udders and a house. It was a real house made of stone, not mud and bark, with six chimneys and a swing out the front and a child on it, all in white frills, and she was pushing the swing, back and forth and back and forth, and somehow she knew that the child was her sister but she couldn't have a sister, she couldn't, not now Mama was dead, and they'd never have a house like this, not in this horrible strange country and ...

Something bumped her leg. Mary Anne opened her eyes.

A monster* blinked up at her. It was the size of a dog, but its legs were shorter, and its thick square body was brown and furry. It had two heads, one at each end of its body. One head blinked at her from tiny slits of eyes, while the other head was eating grass, tearing it up, chomp, chomp, chomp.

It was pretty small for a monster. But what normal animal had two heads?

The monster's first head blinked again then bent to eat grass like the other one. 'If I'm very, very quiet,' thought Mary Anne, 'maybe it'll just eat grass and not eat me.'

Chomp, chomp, chomp ... suddenly the smaller head gave a wriggle and the monster broke in two:

* A wombat. Wombat pouches face backwards (a very good design feature if your mum is a burrowing animal and you don't want a bed full of grit and gravel and sand) so the babies can look out of the pouch and graze at the same time as the mother.

one big monster and a tiny one that squirmed out between the big monster's hind legs.

A mother monster and a baby one, thought Mary Anne. The baby must have been in the mother's pouch underneath its body! Mrs Hanrahan had told her animals in this land had pouches but she hadn't said they'd look so silly! She tried not to giggle.

The baby looked around, bored. It bounced at a shadow, then looked round for something else to do.

Bang! the sound echoed across the valley. Papa must have fired at something, thought Mary Anne. But the monsters just blinked and thought for a second, and then ignored the sound.

The mother monster was itchy. She scratched her back with her hind foot then trundled down to the sand and wriggled into it, as though to say: 'Ah, that's nice and scratchy.'

The baby monster sniffed at Mary Anne's foot. It must be a pretty smelly foot, thought Mary Anne, but the baby monster didn't seem to mind. It butted her again, just as the mother monster stood up, the gleaming sand falling off her and shining in the sunlight ...

'A fine fat duck!' yelled Papa through the trees. 'Just sitting there waiting for our dinner!'

The mother monster froze. The baby monster dashed over to her, then suddenly they were gone, racing surprisingly quickly through the trees.

'What's so funny?' Papa threw the duck down onto the ground then sat down to pluck it.

'There was a baby animal and its mother too, all brown and furry ...'

'That'd be native badgers\*,' said Papa. 'There's some that live in trees and eat gum leaves\*\* and some that live in holes and eat grass.'

'These ate grass. The baby one sniffed my foot and the big one rolled in the sand and came up all sparkling like someone had dusted it with gold, and then...' Mary Anne stopped. 'What is it Papa?'

'Gold,' said Papa slowly. 'It rolled in the sand and came out covered in gold?'

'Not covered, just sort of sparkly and ...'

Papa leapt to his feet. He rummaged in the packs and came up with a tin plate, and carried it down to the sand. Mary Anne ran after him. He shoved a handful of sand onto the plate then dipped it in the water.

He rolled the plate back and forth so most of the sand splashed out with the water. 'There,' said Papa softly. 'Look at that, darling.'

Mary Anne looked. There at the bottom of the dish, among the dull white sand were shiny flakes of ...

'Gold,' whispered Papa. 'Gold!' Suddenly he leapt to his feet. 'Gold,' he yelled. 'You've found us gold!'

He swept Mary Anne off her feet and swung her round and round. 'Gold! Gold! Gold! We'll pan ourselves a bucketful before we tell anyone, then we'll find James and make a claim and ...'

Mary Anne tried to catch her breath. What was gold? Just glittery grains in the sand. But gold made you rich, it gave you a proper house and fruit trees and ...

Somewhere in the shadows the native badgers seemed to grin at her through the trees.

\* wombats  \*\* koalas

27

Slab huts gave you a quick roof over your head and could be made just with what grew around you in the bush. All you needed was an axe, though a shovel would help too.

First, four big upright posts were dug into the ground, then 'slabs' split from other logs were fitted longways into slots cut in the uprights. The gaps between the slabs were filled with clay, and the inside was sometimes plastered, or papered over with newspaper and flour and water glue to help keep out draughts. You could have a read while you had tea! The roof was either sheets of bark, laid across more poles that were tied to the walls with green kangaroo skin that tightened as it dried, or 'shingles' — thin slabs of wood split from large logs, that overlapped like roof tiles.

A 'wattle and daub' hut was even simpler: two posts were placed close together at each corner and 'wattle' — thin saplings sometimes of wattle and sometimes from other trees — slipped in between them. Again, when the wall was 'full', mud or clay was used to fill up the cracks. Clay by itself usually shrank as it dried and fell out, but if you mixed it with dried grass or horsehair, it held its shape for longer.

Mud, of course, washed away in the rain, but if the roof eaves were wide enough, only a wild storm would wash a hole in the walls, and it was soon filled up again.

## 1853 – 1860

Gold mining stripped the valley of its trees, its animals and much of its soil. Trees were cut down for firewood and timber to prop up mines and to make room for tents and shacks.

The lagoons had gone now. Instead there was mud and dams and drifts of sand, and a trickle of water that became a flood when it rained heavily and turned the whole valley into a churning mass of mud and froth.

Forty thousand people from most of the countries of the world crammed into the valley now: Polish, Swiss, Russian, French, Maori, American, both white and black. The Chinese also sought the wealth of 'Hsin Chin san' or 'the Golden Mountain' as they called Australia. They walked in single file to the valley in their wide straw hats and pigtails, their belongings suspended on bamboo poles.

Nearly all were men — there were very few Chinese families, as most of the Chinese miners were indentured labourers. Their masters (often war lords) kept their families back in China to reduce the chances of their absconding.

Unlike most of the other miners — except those who'd come from the Californian gold diggings — the Chinese actually knew how to mine for gold. They sifted the mullock heaps the earlier miners had discarded; they built stone walls to shore up the creek banks as they worked, and constructed giant 'water races' which stretched for kilometres across the hills to bring water from high in the valley to the dry hills and gullies and wash the gold from the soil. (A hundred and fifty years later many of the water races still circle the hills. Some took more than three years to build.)

Partly because the Chinese were such successful miners and partly because there were so many speaking and dressing in a way that seemed foreign to the European settlers (at one stage a third of the people in the valley were Chinese) many miners bitterly resented them, and even petitioned the Governor of New South Wales to have all the Chinese expelled from the colony:

'Your petitioners believe the existence of the Chinese in large numbers in this colony to be a great evil, and are fearful that unless the evil remain uncorrected, the future interests of this portion of Her Majesty's dominions will suffer greatly, being aliens in morals, blood, country and religion ... '

The valley was a place of mud and mines, bare hills and grog shops. There were few women. Each time it rained, the valley became a flood of froth and sand that carried a little new gold down from the hills. But by 1860 most of the gold had been taken.

# 1863

## THE GOLDEN WALLS

The valley smelt of flood and mud and cold. Below him the whole world thundered with the drumbeat of the water.

Sam stood on the hill and watched the flood. He'd seen other floods before, but not like this. It was as though the whole valley floor shivered with an earthquake. You would never have known that two days ago the valley was a maze of men and tents, of mining works and cradles, endlessly washing the river sand to find the gold.

Everything was gone. How many men had drowned, he wondered, when the flood swept through the valley as the rain poured down across the hills? He shivered at the thought of boulders bouncing in the floodwaters, the angry water closing over him, tangling him in tents and trees, and the water so cold, cold, cold …

What would they see when the flood went down? he wondered. Maybe it would be as though men had never mined here. But no, the valley would be brown with mud when the flood went down, not green.

He sighed and began to wander up the valley, watching the frothing water tear boulders from the banks and lash trees around the bends.

What was that? A tent, maybe. And there went a cow, its legs in the air, its body swollen.

It was good to have a holiday from rocking the mining cradle with Dad, anyway. There'd be no more gold panning till the flood went down. Maybe the flood would wash more gold out of the hills. There was precious little gold to find these days. They'd come too late, Dad had said. They were lucky to find five shillings worth of gold a week now.

What must it have been like in the early days, thought Sam, ten years ago when there were fortunes to be found in the gold-rich sand?

The river yelled and raged below him, sweeping around the casuarina trees that had lined the riverbanks two days ago. The world was filled with the smell of the flood, the roar of water ...

Something stopped him. A sound. Like a bird's cry, he thought, but different.

Sam peered across the floodwaters. There was something in that tree. A bit of blue cloth, perhaps, washed up against a tree trunk. Or ...

No, it was impossible! It couldn't be!

But it was.

Sam took one final look. And then he ran.

⌒

The warmth from the fire hit him as he flung open the door. Their walls might be just mud and wattle and the floor beaten earth, but at least the hut was warm and smelt like home.

'Sam! What is it?' Ma looked round from stirring the pot on the fire.

'There's a little girl! In the flood!'

'You saw her washed away! Oh, Sam, how terrible!'

'No!' Sam gasped for breath. 'She's tied to a tree! And the flood is all around her!'

'Tied to a tree! You mean she's still alive?'

'Yes! Ma, we've got to save her, we've got to.'

But Ma was already running out the door. 'Michael!' she yelled. 'Michael!'

Dad looked up from the potato patch, where he was chipping weeds in the soft wet soil. 'What is it?'

'Come now! Run! Hurry!' Ma turned to Sam. 'Go fetch the Schmidt boys. Tell them to bring ropes and axes! Hurry boy! Hurry!'

The floodwater had retreated just a little. A strip of mud and foam lined the hills where it had been. But the tree with the girl still stood at least three metres out in the raging water.

Sam's Dad stared up at it. 'Holy crows!' he muttered, and for once Sam's Ma didn't tick him off for swearing. 'It *is* a child ...'

'Who tied her there?' demanded Sam.

Ma shivered. 'Poor lamb, poor lamb. Her parents must have been washed against the tree as the water rose. Maybe they clung there till their arms grew too tired to hold them. They must have tied her to the trunk to keep her safe.'

Ma shut her eyes briefly at the thought of the cold water then opened them again. 'We have to save her,' she said firmly. 'Heaven knows how long she's been there in the wet and cold.'

'But how? that is the question,' said Ernst Schmidt in his heavy Prussian accent, looking doubtfully at the brown and swirling water. 'If we are trying into that to wade, missus, we are being swept away! Mebbe it's waiting we should be, till down it goes some more.'

'If we wait, the poor lamb will die of cold, and terror too! You two,' she nodded at the Schmidt boys, 'you cut down the tallest tree you can — a thin one mind, long enough to reach that tree!'

⌒

The sharp song of the axes rang across the crash of the flood. The child had stopped crying now. She hung limp against the rough bark of the casaurina.

Craaaack ... the gum tree crashed onto the sodden ground, taking a young wattle with it. The axes rang again as Dad and the Schmidts trimmed off the branches.

'Hurry!' called Ma, her eyes still on the child in the water. 'You're slow as a wet Monday! We're coming, love,' she yelled across the water. But the child in the tree was still.

Dad and the Schmidts carried the pole down to the river.

'Wedge it between the boulders!' ordered Ma. 'That's it. Now ease it out up here.'

The pole crashed down into the water then disappeared. Suddenly it floated again, and Sam

realised what Ma had planned. One end of the pole was anchored on the bank. The other swept against the child's tree and lodged there, forming a bridge between the shore and the tree.

But what a bridge! It bobbed and washed in the flood, sometimes above water and sometimes below. It would never take anyone's weight, thought Sam, even if the child was able to untie herself.

Dad took off his boots and then his shirt and trousers till he stood there just in the combinations that Ma had knitted for him and insisted he wear in wet weather to keep off the rheumatics.

'No,' whispered Sam. 'Dad, you can't ...'

His father bent and hugged him, then hugged Ma too. Then he lifted his arms for the Schmidts to tie their thick rope under his shoulders. Dad picked up a smaller rope and looped it and tied it with a swift, loose knot. He held it firmly as he began to wade into the water.

One step, two ... the water swirled around his knees. The muddy foam flecked his combinations. Four steps, five — and suddenly the flood gripped him and cast him down so he sank beneath the water.

'Dad!' screamed Sam, but even as he spoke Dad's head bobbed up, his arms holding onto the tree as it bobbed in the water. Slowly, impossibly slowly, he began to inch his way along, one arm holding on while the other searched for a new handhold. Nearer ... nearer ... nearer ... Around him the water swirled and bubbled. A log burst to the surface. For a moment Sam thought it would strike

Dad, but another eddy took it bobbing away through the foam.

'Gott in Himmel!' whispered Ernst. 'No man can swim through that.'

'Don't say die till a dead horse kicks you!' hissed Ma. 'You hold your tongue!'

Dad reached out his hand and caught the casuarina tree. For a long moment he seemed to try to catch his breath, then one hand reached up for the ropes that held the child and began to struggle with the knots.

Suddenly the child collapsed into his arms, and they were gone, both of them, beneath the wild brown water. But almost instantly Dad's head bobbed up again. He still held the child. For a moment he struggled to slip the rope around her body and his. Then the knot lashed close, and they were tied together. He reached out for the floating tree trunk. The water washed over them once more.

'Grab the trunk and keep it steady, you great buffoons!' screamed Ma. She grabbed the rope from the Schmidt boys and pulled it hard to keep it taut. Sam and the Schmidts grasped the tree trunk and tried to hold it up, out of the water.

They were only partially successful, but it was enough for Dad to inch his way across again, handhold by handhold, till finally Ernst could wade into the water and grab the child as Dad undid the slip knot. Sam waded into the flood too, to help Dad as he staggered into shore.

'Didn't I know he'd do it!' muttered Ma, almost to herself. 'And him the strongest, loveliest man in the whole valley.' And then she was running, to take the child from Ernst's arms, while Dad sagged on the sodden grass, the breath heaving back into his lungs.

The child was still alive, though her face was blue with cold. Even the rough trot up the hill to home didn't wake her. Ma ordered Dad and Sam from the hut as soon as they had changed their clothes and stripped her down and dried her and wrapped her in her own red flannel nightdress, and then into her shawl and then into Sam's bed (a straw mattress on rough-cut palings between two logs of wood) with both feather quilts on top of her.

Ma was just throwing more wood onto the fire when Sam and Dad peered in. 'Can we help?' asked Dad.

Ma nodded. 'You can sit down and get something warm inside you. It'll do none of us any good if you get your death of cold. And you too,' she ordered Sam, as she slid one of the hot rocks by the fire onto the spade, then wrapped it in flannel and shoved it near the girl's feet to warm them.

'There you are, lambkin,' she said. 'Snug as a bug in a rug.'

The stew was mostly potatoes and cabbage from the garden, with a bit of salt mutton from the barrel by the door to give it flavour. (The last fresh meat they'd eaten had been at Christmas when Dad had shot a roo, but you had to walk a long, hard way up the valley now to find game.) But the stew was hot and comforting. Ma scooped out some of the liquid and sat on a stool by the bed, spooning minute drops into the girl's mouth.

'She's swallowing,' she whispered. 'That's a good sign at least.'

'How old do you think she is?'

'About four maybe,' said Ma, considering.

'But who is she?' asked Dad.

Ma shrugged. With forty thousand people, near enough, from half the nations of the world, camped in the valley, the chances were they'd never find out who the child belonged to.

'She looks a bit Chinee,' said Sam. 'The way her eyes go.'

'Maybe her Dad's Chinee,' said Ma.

The Chinese miners kept mostly to themselves, taking claims abandoned by other miners. They worked carefully and patiently and used their greater engineering skills to find the flakes hidden from others. Some constructed water races — kilometre after kilometre of ditches in hills and wooden piping across gullies — to bring water to the higher ground where no one had bothered to look for gold because there was no water with which to pan it.

Ma shook her head. 'You go down into the valley,' she ordered Dad. 'And see if anyone claims her. Can't be too many Chinee children here.'

After lunch Dad wandered down the valley, with fresh combinations, that Ma had warmed for him by the fire, under his shirt and trousers. Sam kept the fire high with dry twigs and chips split off the larger logs and in between, cut new poles to make another bed.

'Not that I can make another mattress till the bracken dries,' said Ma. 'You'll have to sleep in our bed tonight.'

Sam nodded. He looked down at the child. Her face was no longer blue and her breathing was stronger.

'I think she'll do,' said Ma softly, and there was a softness in her face that Sam rarely saw. 'I think she'll do.'

~

No one had heard of a lost Chinese child down the valley; if indeed she *was* Chinese. 'For that Russian man had eyes a bit like that,' said Ma. 'And one of them Afghan traders that came last year, his eyes were different too.'

The child woke the next morning. Sam opened his eyes, and there she was, staring at him, her brown eyes wide as she sat up in his bed.

Sam nudged Ma. 'Ma, she's awake!' he hissed.

'Wha ... ?' Ma brushed away sleep. 'She is too!' Instantly she was out of bed and at the child's side, feeling her forehead for fever.

'It's a miracle,' she breathed. 'Look at her, bright as a button. Well, child, and what's your name then?'

The child stared at her.

'This is Sam,' said Ma slowly. 'And you can call me Ma and this is Dad.'

The brown eyes blinked, but still the child said nothing.

'Maybe she only speaks Chinee,' offered Dad.

'Maybe,' said Ma doubtfully. 'You go and find Ah Ping the grocer and see if he can talk to her. I have my doubts though.' She gave the girl one of her rare smiles. 'Are you warm enough, lambkin?'

The girl nodded.

'See?' declared Ma. 'I reckon she understands me well enough.'

'Do you think she's dumb then?' asked Sam.

Ma hugged the girl's shoulders fiercely. 'Dumb? Of course she's not dumb. Just shocked, more like. You find yourself tied to a tree in a flood and see your parents washed away and see how much you feel like chattering!'

It seemed Ma was right. Ah Ping came up, but the child made no sound when he spoke to her. Dad hauled Dr Carruthers up from O'Halloran's grog shop, too; he was mostly sober as it was still morning.

Dr Carruthers smelt of rum and sweat. He scratched his chin. 'No reason she can't speak that I can see,' he said. 'Are you going to keep her then?'

'Of course we're going to keep her!' flared Ma. 'Unless her family claims her,' she amended.

'Well, I'll ask around,' said Dr Carruthers, glancing longingly out the door at the track that led to the grog shop. 'Now if there's nothing more you're wanting, missus ...'

Ma shut the door behind him, though the smell of stale rum still filled the room. 'Not worth his weight in rocking horse dirt,' she declared.

Sam sat on the bed by the girl. 'It's funny,' he said. 'We don't even know her name.'

'It's Florence,' said Ma shortly.

Sam stared. 'How do you know?'

'Because I had an Aunt Florrie, that's why. Now you go and help your dad dig the ground for the winter cabbages. I don't know — cluttering the place up. Be off with you!' But she pressed a slice of bread and sugar into his hand as he left.

So Florrie stayed.

For the first week she mostly lay in bed, wide-eyed and staring. But at least she ate. Ma spooned bread and water into her at first, then stew and soup, then sent Sam searching for wild raspberries in the gullies. And slowly Florrie's eyes lost their wide and frightened look, till one day she hugged Ma and kissed Sam splodgily on the cheek when he brought her the doll he'd made for her out of sticks and scraps of cloth.

But still she didn't speak. She never smiled either. But who could expect the child to smile, Ma said, after all that she'd been through?

The valley was returning to normal now — if a chaos of mud and men and the creaks of windlasses and shouts in two dozen languages could ever be called normal. The river fell back to its normal muddy self, and soon even the smell of flood was gone, and new tents rose along its banks.

Life returned to normal too. Sometimes it seemed to Sam as though Florrie had always been with them, helping Ma to scrub the potatoes or hang the washing up, or even panning for gold down at the river's edge with him and Dad.

'And a good little panner she is too,' said Dad approvingly, watching her swirl the water in her pan, and Florrie sent him a look from her dark brown eyes and chewed the end of the fat black plait that Ma tied up for her each morning.

Sam had thought she might be scared of the river. But instead she seemed happy there, as though her good memories of the river outweighed her bad.

Six weeks later the clouds blew in green and purple from the coast, and it rained again, a wild lash of water as though someone was pouring buckets down from the clouds, and the river flooded a second time, taking tents and tools, pumps and barrows in a wild roar of water. But this time at least everyone had moved to higher ground in time and no lives were lost.

'Well, not from the flood anyway,' said Ma grimly, surveying the devastation below their shack. 'Though it'll be a hard and hungry winter now.'

She sighed. 'Well, what can't be cured must be endured. At least we have spuds enough and cabbages and a roof over our heads, even if the rain drips through the bark sometimes. There's enough who don't even have that. And at least we didn't have a pump to wash away. The less you have; the less you have to lose.'

Which was no comfort at all, thought Sam. But he didn't say anything.

Many miners left after the second flood, moving up to the new diggings at Kiandra. Most of those that stayed had richer claims, or mines up in the gullies, or shacks and a family like Sam's.

But it was a hard winter, despite Ah Ping giving

credit at the store for flour and sugar and a twist of tea to keep the family going. Ma's face grew grimmer and Dad's more worried.

'You know, love, we'll just have to face it,' he said to Ma one night, as she served the stew at the rough wood table. 'The gold in the river is mostly gone. There's no gold here unless you mine for it, and it's twenty shillings a month rent and money in advance to pay for a claim, and the pumps to get the water out and batteries to crush the rock. And with my luck it'd be a dud claim anyway,' he added wryly.

'What do you want us to do then?' asked Ma warily.

'We'll have to leave the valley. I'll have to look for work somewhere. Something with horses mebbe. I've always had a hankering to work with horses.'

'Leave my house?' It may have been just a shack to others, but to Ma it was a palace. 'And what do we feed the family on while we go wandering off without a roof over our heads?'

'You all stay here,' said Dad, 'till I can find a job and send for you. A few weeks, that's all it would be.'

'I...' began Ma, then stopped. 'Florrie, love, what is it?'

The child's chair crashed down behind her. She stood wide-eyed for a second, then ran from the shack.

'Sam, go after her!' cried Ma.

Sam ran down the track. Where was she going? Down the valley or up into the hills? No, there she was, heading to the river.

He stopped, for Florrie had stopped too. The thin arms clasped the casuarina tree where they'd found her.

Sam walked forward slowly. 'Florrie ... Florrie, it's alright.'

Florrie shook her head, so her plait bounced on her shoulders. Tears crept from her eyes.

'You don't want to leave the valley, do you? Neither do I. But we're not going yet. Really.'

Florrie clasped the tree even tighter.

'Is it ...?' Sam stopped. He wanted to ask, is it because you lost your parents here? Do you think if we stay in the valley you might find them again? Or have you lost so much you don't want to lose any more?

But he didn't. The valley was all he could remember too. If he said anything, he was afraid he would begin to cry as well.

He unclenched her hands gently and lifted her up. She clung to him fiercely, like a native bear in skirts. They walked up the track together.

⁓

Dad left next morning. There was no point delaying, Ma said, and getting further into debt at Ah Ping's. Best to get it over with and, God willing, he'd soon find a place where he could send for them and send them some money too, to pay off Ah Ping and pay a carter to carry their bits and pieces in his cart.

Sam watched Dad walk up the track, his swag on his back, the billy bouncing with each step. Ma's face was strangely expressionless as she stood in the doorway beside him. Florrie shivered and took Sam's hand.

'Best come in,' said Ma abruptly. 'The child's cold.'

She shut the door, so they could no longer see Dad

growing smaller in the distance, and pushed the kettle closer to the fire. 'We'll feel better when we've got a cup of tea inside us,' she added.

'Ma?'

'Yes?' Ma didn't turn round.

'You don't want to go, do you?'

'No choice,' said Ma tightly. 'A woman follows her man and that's that. Besides, there's nothing for us here. There never has been.'

'But ... but Dad might have found gold, lots of gold ...'

Ma said nothing, and suddenly Sam realised she was crying. But Ma never cried.

'I wish ...' he began.

Suddenly Ma raised her face from the fire. 'Put a wish in one hand and spit in the other, and see which is full first!' she cried fiercely. 'Ah, your father's a great one for wishing too! "We'll find gold!" he said to me. "Great lovely nuggets of it, darling. You'll have a house with an iron stove and glass in all the windows." But it never happened. It was just a dream, and now we have to pay for it.'

Sam glanced at Florrie. She was staring at Ma. I bet she understands everything, thought Sam. He crossed over to Ma and put his hand on her shoulder. 'Ma ...' he began.

'Ah, leave me be for a while,' said Ma. 'I've got the pip, that's all. Gold fever, they call it. Well, it's a fever right enough. A sickness in the head ...'

Sam nodded helplessly. He pulled Florrie's plait. 'Come on, chicken. Let's go down to the river and do some panning, just us two. Maybe we'll make our fortunes yet.'

But he could hear Ma's sobs as they walked down the track.

～

The wall disappeared that night.

Not the whole wall, of course. There was just a hole by the back door when they woke in the morning, as wide as a wheelbarrow maybe, with the winter wind gusting through it.

Ma stared at the hole. 'Great loaves and little fishes!' she exclaimed. 'What could have done it?'

'A badger,' suggested Sam.

'What badger would want to tunnel through our wall?'

'Maybe it was cold and wanted to come inside.'

Ma snorted. 'And where's all the dirt then? A badger would have left a proper mess.' She shook her head. 'After all that's happened to us, now someone's stealing our wall too.'

'I'll stack some firewood against it to keep the wind out,' said Sam. 'It's not worth repairing. We'll be gone soon.' He stopped when he saw Ma's face.

But she just said, 'Thank you, Sam,' and shoved the bread into the Dutch oven for their breakfast.

But it was strange, thought Sam, as he and Florrie shook the hard white sand in their pans later that day. Why would anyone want to destroy their wall? It wouldn't be a burglar because there was nothing to steal, and anyway, a burglar could just come through the door.

It must have been a joke, he decided. Someone had ...

Florrie pulled at his shirt then tugged it again when he failed to look at her.

'I wish you'd learn to talk,' he told her. 'Then you could say "Pardon me, Sir Samuel".'

He'd hoped to make her smile, but she didn't. She just tugged at his shirt again and lifted up her pan towards him. Sam peered into it. Two or three flakes of gold clung to the sides, almost too small to see.

Sam took the gold jar out of his pocket and unscrewed the lid, then wet his fingers and pressed them down on the flakes and transferred them to the jar. They must have a whole sixpence worth in there now, he reckoned. Poor enough pay for two days work. But every little helped, as the farmer said when he widdled in the well.

He smiled down at Florrie. 'You're a great little gold panner,' he told her. 'I bet your ma and pa showed you how to do it, eh?'

Florrie didn't respond. It was almost as though she hadn't heard. She just dipped her pan in the sand again and then in the water and began to shake and turn it.

Sam gazed at her. There were shadows around her eyes. 'You really don't want to leave the valley, do you?' Sam asked softly.

Florrie looked up. She shook her head then bent down again to her panning.

'Well, I don't either,' said Sam. 'And nor does Ma. Or Dad either come to that. But maybe, maybe Pa will find a good place. And then you'll learn to smile again and Ma will be happy.'

But he'll have to work all day, Sam thought. I won't be able to spend all day with him panning or weeding the vegetables or stacking firewood. He bit his lip and filled his dish with sand again.

It was hard to get to sleep that night, despite the hard day's panning. Sam lay awake, listening to the owl booming away up the gorge and the shouts from below, as drunken miners staggered back from O'Halloran's pub or one of the tents that sold stomach-rot rum and hooch.

Would whoever — whatever — had put the hole in their wall come back again?

But of course they wouldn't, thought Sam. There was no reason to put one hole in their wall, much less another one. It was just some silly prank.

He shut his eyes. The next thing he knew, Ma had her shawl wrapped around her nightdress and was exclaiming, 'Good gravy! That jumped up son of a sea-cook has done it again!'

Sam sat up and stared at the gum leaves blowing through the hole in the wall, twice as large as it was the day before.

⌒

They sat at the table and discussed it.

'Maybe it's a mouse!' suggested Sam.

'A mouse that big would eat the food safe, door and all,' snorted Ma, and Florrie gave an almost smile. 'No, it's some big fool down the valley has done it. Maybe they think as we're leaving, we don't need our walls. Well, I'll tell you something, tonight I'm staying awake even if it kills me. I'm going to catch whoever's doing this and give them a piece of my mind!'

Sam decided to stay awake too. But it was difficult. He watched the fire for a while, slowly sinking into its bed of coals, and then watched Ma, upright in her chair with her eyes on the back wall. But slowly he grew more and more tired. Till finally he shut his eyes, just for a second.

The next thing he knew the kookaburras were yelling, and there was Ma dozing open-mouthed in her chair, and Florrie fast asleep in the bed near the fire.

And the hole in the wall was no bigger than it had been the day before.

⌒

So there was no need to stay awake on the third night.

'Which is just as well,' said Ma wearily. 'A herd of cows could run through the place tonight and I wouldn't open my eyes. Here Florrie, love, elbows off the table when you're eating. Do you want people to think you were brought up in a barn?'

Night settled slowly on the valley — the sun sinking behind the ridges by mid-afternoon as it always did in winter, the shadows merging together as though the light drifted away from the valley with the river — till suddenly you realised you could see the stars and the possums were yelling up in the hills.

It was potato cakes for dinner, thick with chopped cabbage and onions and bits of bacon that Ah Ping had slipped into the package with the flour when he'd heard that Dad had gone.

Ma made the best potato cakes in the world, thought Sam, as he pulled his quilt over his head to keep out the draft from the hole in the wall. Even Florrie had eaten four. He drifted into a dream where Dad came home with a sackful of potato cakes and ...

Something moved across the room. Sam opened his eyes and peered slowly over the quilt. A white shape fluttered in the darkness, over by the door.

For a terrifying moment Sam thought it was a ghost. Maybe Florrie's parents had come to haunt them. But they'd be glad, surely, that another family had taken their daughter in. Or maybe it was the ghosts of the black fellers who'd been driven out when the miners came. Or ...

No, it was no ghost. It was a nightdress, the old white one that Ma had cut down for Florrie.

Sam wriggled out from under the quilt. His bare feet made no sound on the hard dirt floor. He touched Ma's arm.

'Wha ... ?' began Ma.

'Shh,' he whispered in her ear. 'It's Florrie.'

Ma sat up, instantly alert. She pulled her boots on quietly then followed Sam out the door.

The stars winked up in the black sky. The moon seemed to shiver in the cold. Florrie shivered too in her thin nightdress, huddled by the hole in the wall.

'What's wrong, lambkin?' asked Ma softly. Then she stopped.

Sam stared too.

Florrie's small hand held a pointed stick. The other held her gold pan, half full of dirt from the wall.

'Oh, the dear child,' said Ma quietly. 'She's thinking to help us by panning at night too! Come in child, before you catch your death out here. Sam, clean that mess away will you? No, don't bother now, morning will do.' She bent to pick Florrie up.

'Ma, stop,' said Sam suddenly.

'What?' She looked where Sam was pointing, down at the gold pan and at the jar beside it.

The jar was almost full. Even in the moonlight the gold shone bright.

'She's found gold in the walls,' whispered Sam. 'There's gold in our walls!' He stared up at Ma. 'They were built right at the beginning of the rush, weren't they? When there was lots of gold about! And there was gold in the mud too! Ma! Ma, we've got a golden house!'

Ma's legs seemed to give way. She sat down abruptly on the cold ground and pulled Florrie onto her lap. 'I don't believe it! We're ... we're rich!' she said. 'Florrie ... Florrie, how did you know?'

'Her dad was a miner,' said Sam. 'A *really* good miner. Wasn't he, Florrie?'

Florrie looked up at him, her arms around Ma's neck. 'Gold,' she said. 'Lots and lots of gold!' And then she smiled, and her smile was brighter than the moon.

# How to Pan for Gold

The simplest way to find gold is to pan for it with a shallow metal dish that has a wide edge to it, though any bowl can be used at a pinch.

First blacken your dish so the gold will shine against it. Place the dish above your fire — or in an oven — and heat it till it darkens. Don't let smoke blacken it though — soot makes the gold flakes greasy and when you put water in later the greasy flakes will float and you will lose them when you tip the water out.

The best place to look for gold bearing sand or gravel is at bends of creeks or rivers. As gold is heavier than sand it tends to sink wherever the water slows down at bends, or where the creek or river flows more slowly at the edges.

Another good place to find gold is where a creek or river stops racing down a mountain and slows down and flattens out. Again, as the water slows down, the gold will settle in beds of sand or gravel. Sometimes you'll find gold gathered behind rocky bars or logs too.

Half fill your dish with sand and gravel. Now dip your dish in the water till it's full and lift it up again. Begin to rock it gently back and forth, then round and round, then back and forth again. As you rock, the heavier gold will slowly sink to the bottom.

Once you've rocked and swirled for five minutes or so, tip the dish slowly while shaking it from side to side so that most of the water and maybe half the top sand and gravel floats out. You must keep shaking as you tip so that only the top stuff falls out.

Add more water and keep shaking and rocking, and now and then slip out a bit more water and rubbish. When about another half of your sand and gravel has gone, pick out any large bits of gravel with your fingers. Look at them carefully, as they may contain bits of gold or have flakes of gold sticking to them. If so, put the gold in your jar.

Keep adding more water to the gold pan and tipping out the stuff on top, until about half a cupful of sand and gravel is left. Now pour out as much water as you can — make sure there are no flakes of gold in it. Pick out the flecks of gold with a wet finger; they'll stick to it. Very practised gold panners can pan right down till there's nothing but gold left, but this takes a long time to get right!

Now put the flakes of gold into a jar and put the lid on. Get another dish of sand and gravel and start all over again!

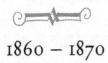

# 1860 – 1870

Gradually the chaos of the early mining days settled down into some sort of order. Tents became shacks, shacks became houses, grog shops became pubs and tracks turned into roads.

Life became more comfortable. There was even a road down the steep slopes into the valley now, and supplies were no longer slid in barrels down muddy slopes, to crash open against the trees below. Bullock drays carted in barrels of flour and beer and sugar, and 'Syrian traders' led pack horses laden with bolts of material for clothes and sheets, and saucepans and plates and lanterns.

The valley now had a football club and a cricket club. There was even a school, where the teacher was paid pennies by the parents, though the first teacher was too drunk most days to teach. The second was better and the children learnt their letters and their numbers, first of all in a canvas tent and then in a hut built by the parents, though in winter it was so cold they couldn't hold their slates.

There was a post office now in the valley, too. But there was no police station yet, nor any banks. A passenger coach pulled by four horses travelled to Sydney every day except Sunday, and every two weeks the gold was shipped by coach up the narrow road through the ridges to the township thirty miles away, with an armed escort for protection. The owners of the coach service were paid £1850 a year. (A good cook earnt £60 a year and their keep — the owners of the coach service were well paid!)

And now there were bushrangers too.

The earliest bushrangers were mostly escaped convicts, but sons of poor farmers also turned to bushranging. There were no schools for farmers' kids in those days, and magistrates and police were often corrupt, seizing farms and other goods. Bushrangers usually couldn't read or write and had no faith in the so-called justice system around them. They were mostly poor, uneducated, young men, who turned to theft and violence in desperation.

Many small farmers and miners were sympathetic to bushrangers. Bushrangers mainly targeted the wealthy — partly because they had more to steal, but also because most bushrangers came from the poor farming class themselves. Even when a small farmer didn't actively help a bushranger, they'd probably not turn them in.

It's easy to think the bushranger's life was romantic. It wasn't. Their lives were dangerous and short. They were forced to camp away from comfort, hunted (so they had to avoid towns), and they never knew when the next coach would bring an ambush. A few bushrangers escaped to other colonies when they'd had enough of stealing. All died poor. Most of them died young in prison.

A bushranger's horse was more valuable than his pistol. The horses had to be good (fast and with exceptional stamina), not scared of sudden noise and able to cover eighty or ninety miles in twenty-four hours, down gullies and up hills.

Nearly everyone had a horse in those days — you had to be really hard up to go on foot. Most people in the country owned a saddle horse; even maids had a saddle and a bridle and a horse in the paddock that they'd ride to church on Sundays.

Feed usually cost nothing, unless a horse was being worked hard: most horses were just turned out into the paddocks at night. (A horse is a heck of a lot cheaper to run than a car.) Even at the height of the gold rush, there were paddocks of corn growing in the valley to feed the horses.

A cheap horse — and most horses were cheap — cost between one and four pounds. A really good horse, though, could cost hundreds of pounds — or even thousands — and those were the horses a bushranger needed.

# 1865

## The night of the bushranger

My mother was mostly Timor pony. (Her mother remembered the journey here from Timor — the smell of salt, damp wood and musty hay stayed with her all her life.)

My father was a scrubber or brumby — one of those wild bush horses that hide in gullies or thick timber, stealing out into the cleared paddocks at night for grass and water. He and his mares were rounded up and captured, and soon after that he met my mother and the result was me. Later he was roughly broken in and sold cheap to Cobb and Co.

It was a hard life for a horse with Cobb and Co, travelling day and night through rain or drought, anything from a ten to a forty-mile run before the horses were changed, depending on how steep the climb and poor the track. The horses died in harness mostly, and were cut from the traces and dragged to the side of the track. There they lay, food for the goannas and the crows that pecked their bones.

I'm telling you all this so you understand what sort of horse I am — what they called a steady goer.

I have a tummy like a roly-poly pudding (in good seasons) and my neck's a bit too short. A good enough horse, but not the sort you'd ever expect a bushranger to ride.

The bushranger's horse was king. You had to be fast to be a bushranger's horse but you had to have endurance too. You had to ride hard all day and then through the night, keeping just in front of the police horses that were never quite as good as you.

How could they be? The police had to buy their horses. The bushrangers simply took the best, riding into some isolated farm, reins in one hand and pistol in the other and a second pistol in their belt. They'd take their time choosing the best horses and take the best saddles too.

Bushrangers like race horses or well-bred stockhorses, with lots of thoroughbred blood in them for speed and a dash of Arab for endurance: bred for the chase.

There is another quality a bushranger's horse has to have as well. They have to have courage: to stand firm when pistols fire about them, to keep their head and dodge the branches among the heavy timber, with a gang of troopers on their heels.

I am not like that at all.

I was a postie's horse or I was for two days a fortnight anyway. Every fortnight the Cobb and Co coach dropped the mail sacks at Coopers' Post Office, next to my paddock. In those days the post office was well up the road from the diggings. Mrs Cooper didn't like the noise or the grog shops, so the miners had to wander up the valley to get their mail, while I carried the mail to the farms.

Once a week Mrs Cooper stuffed the mail I was to carry into my saddlebags, along with a hamper of mutton pie and apple betty and a twist of tea and sugar in the billy for Mr Cooper, then Mr Cooper saddled me.

We took the mail from the post office down through the valley, with the diggings all around. The diggers all knew me there. 'Hello old boy!' they'd call and sometimes pat my flanks.

From there we took the bridle track down to the lower valley, then up to Miller's Creek, all dense scrub cut just wide enough for us to pass. Mr Cooper would lead me through the creek to spare me for the climb ahead while he sang 'Blue Muslin' and 'Annie Laurie' — songs he never sang at home because Mrs Cooper said he had a voice like a bullfrog and no sense of tune.

There were no houses at Miller's Creek but there were a few farms downstream, so we'd leave their mail in the hollow stump on the flat, where a sandy track led in and out among the trees, and wallabies peered at us among the shadows.

Once the creek rose and I had to swim from bank to bank with Mr Cooper on my back, angling across the current, hoping it didn't take us too far downstream, while dodging the floating logs that could drown us both. One winter's night a dingo joined Mr Cooper in his swag too — you'd never seen a man leap so far so fast. But mostly, it was uneventful.

In the early days Mr Cooper hobbled me so I couldn't run away, but later he grew to trust me so he left me free. I think he hoped I'd keep the dingoes away too.

We'd be home again the afternoon of the second day — it was always quicker coming back without the load of mail to carry, and sometimes Mr Cooper picked a bunch of wild bush flowers for Mrs Cooper. She'd have a bin of oats for me and give me a good brush down as well before I was put out in the paddock. There'd be fresh scones with melon jam for Mr Cooper or, in the winter, lemon butter if the hens were laying well.

The rest of the time I had it easy. When they took the buggy down to the church on Sunday mornings, it was mostly Rex and Sam they harnessed up, not me. It was a quiet life, as you can see. There was just Rex and Sam and me in our paddock by the creek; it was a good paddock and always had plenty of grass for the three of us and the wombat, too. We watched the miners during the day when they wandered up to see if someone back home had sent a letter for them, and chased the roos at night when they eyed the grass in our paddock.

That was till the night the bushrangers arrived.

It was a still night the evening that they came. The moon, half-risen, was sending shadows among the trees, black and gold shadows like you only see at night. I was munching the way you do, with a light doze in between.

And then I heard them.

It was the hoof beats first of all, fast and steady down the track.

At first I thought it was the mail coach, though it wasn't due for days. Humans are unpredictable — you never really know what they will do — so I was quite prepared for the coach to come off schedule.

But there was no sound of coach wheels in the night, no creak of springs at all, just the beat of hooves along the road. Two horses coming, I decided, no — three, and one of them was lame.

They came in sight then, down the moonlit road. They were horses like I'd always dreamt of being: tall with arching necks and long proud legs. Their riders leant back into the saddle. They wore leather thongs that held their hats on when they rode fast and scarlet cummerbunds and bright shirts of red and pink and stripes. They were all young men, younger even than the Coopers' sons. Only one was old enough to have a beard.

I thought the lantern would go on inside the house. Surely Mrs Cooper must have heard them! She always woke up first when the fox got at the hens or the night the tree came down. But the windows of the house stayed dark.

The horses were quiet except for the clip clop of their hooves along the road, and the riders were quiet too. I suppose they'd had a lot of practice at being quiet.

They pulled up just by our paddock and the rider of the lame horse dismounted and led his mount over and peered through the fence at us in the moonlight. He looked to be the youngest of them all.

One of the riders, the tallest, said: 'Well, that's it then, Fred. Three of them. Which one will you choose?'

The second rider shook his head. 'None of them's much chop,' he said. His hands were hairy, like a wombat's hide.

The tallest said: 'The big bay's not too bad. Might have a bit of speed in him.'

The big bay was Rex. He was what you might call a showy horse, a thoroughbred who'd failed on the turf. But he didn't have the heart in him that I had, that's what Mr Cooper said anyway, which is why he took me with the post, not Rex. And as for Sam, well, she was a real nark. She was always out to make trouble then snort as soon as she was caught and sidle sideways.

Fred didn't say anything. He just looked at Rex, then he looked at Sam, then he looked at me, then back at Rex again.

Rex lifted his head and whinnied in the moonlight, proud and tall.

Hairy Hands said: 'I say we leave poor Centipede here, and one of us double-backs it. There's sure to be more horses down towards the creek.'

'No time,' said Tallest. 'We'll be hard pressed to catch the coach as it is. Look sharp, young Fred, pick one out.'

He was going to take Rex. I knew he was going to take Rex. I took a step forward and then another. Then Fred said, 'That one!' He pointed straight at me.

Hairy Hands laughed. 'You want your head seeing to, boy! That one won't last! Take the big one!'

'No,' said Fred stubbornly. 'I like this one. I like the look in his eye.'

Tallest sighed. 'Well, it's your lookout,' he said. 'It's your neck they'll stretch if they catch you. Come on, get on with it then! Half the night's gone already.'

Fred opened the gate and led the lame horse in. It was a big chestnut: a true bushranger's horse. Fred clicked his fingers at me and I stepped over smartly. Fred laughed and stroked my neck. 'See how willing he is? You're a good horse, aren't you, Patches, boy?'

Mr Cooper called me Tommy, but what does it matter what humans call you?

Three minutes later the saddle was on me instead of Centipede. It was lighter than the one Mr Cooper used. It felt strange not to have the heavy bags of mail on my back, too. I felt like kicking up my heels. But I didn't. I could feel Rex staring at me and Sam and the lame horse Centipede, but I didn't look their way.

Fred pulled the gate shut again then leapt lightly up onto my back. He was lighter than Mr Cooper, too.

Hairy Hands laughed. 'Don't know what the old couple will say,' he said. 'When they find this weedy fellow has turned into Centipede in the night! They'll think the fairies have been!'

I looked back at Centipede. He looked a fine horse, all flowing neck and lovely lines: a handsome chestnut, shiny-coated in the moonlight, not a patchy piebald like me. But I wondered how Centipede would go slogging through the mud at Miller's Creek, with two bags of heavy mail upon his back, and if he'd know enough to keep the dingoes from Mr Cooper's swag.

Then we were off.

It was just a gentle canter at first. I think they were seeing if I could keep up with them. Well, that was no problem. I could go like that for hours, especially without the mail bags and Mr Cooper's weight to carry.

Up the road at first, away from the diggings, then across country, heading up the valley through the trees. They slowed down for that as the branches were hanging so low that the first rider kept on yelling 'Duck!', but the branches were no trouble to me — the forest at Sawyer's Crossing is twice as thick. Then suddenly Fred pulled at the reins. 'Whoa, Patches, lad,' he whispered, and we were there.

It was just a bend in the road, white in the moonlight with the tree shadows dark across it. But there was good cover where we were. We could see the road, but no one could see us. We were just shadows with the other shadows in the trees.

The riders all dismounted. Fred stroked my neck.

'He kept up alright,' said Tallest grudgingly.

Hairy Hands snorted. 'That little doddle? A poodle could have kept up back there.'

'He's sure-footed,' said Fred. 'Not even winded, see?'

Hairy Hands laughed. 'We'll find a proper mount for you tomorrow, up on the tableland farms,' he promised.

'What's the time, Mike?' Tallest pulled out a handsome timepiece from his pocket. It glinted gold in the moonlight, and I wondered who he'd stolen it from. 'Half an hour till dawn,' he said. 'We made better time than I thought. They'll be here soon.'

We heard them first. Six horses, my ears said, and a coach too, coming up from the diggings. And then we saw it — the cloud of dust, the three reflector lamps bright red beacons in the early light — four horses and the coach.

Only four horses? I thought. I was sure that I'd heard six. But then there was no time to think. The other two were in the saddle, urging their horses forward. Fred spurred me forward too.

It takes courage to stand in the middle of a coaching road with four horses bearing down on you, and the coach behind them too. I never knew how much courage it took till then.

The coach screeched to a halt, the driver swearing and the coach wheels screaming and the horses neighing with fright. Four horses.

I lifted my head and smelt the air. There were more horses somewhere near; I was sure of it. But the boy on my back didn't seem to suspect anything. Sometimes it seems to me that humans only see half the world.

'Stand and deliver!' called Tallest, pistol in one hand and reins in the other. The others had drawn their pistols too.

The driver laughed. 'Well, you've got me bang to rights, lads,' he said. 'The gold's under the seat if you want it.'

'Get it out then and fast about it!' ordered Tallest.

'Surely, surely, keep your hair on,' said the driver. He was still grinning. He moved his legs and the big bag of straw he'd used to keep them warm, and hauled a small trunk out from under the seat. 'It's all yours,' he said.

'Open it!' ordered Tallest.

The driver shook his head. 'Well, that's one thing I can't be obliging you with,' he said, all friendly like.

'Be hanged with you!' yelled Tallest, pulling on the reins in his anger so his horse skittered under him. 'Open that chest, I said!'

The driver held the chest out. 'See, lads, it's locked, you see. But I'm sure fine strong boys like yourselves will have no trouble with it.'

Tallest cantered over and swung the chest up on the saddle in front of him. A woman's face peered out of the coach. Someone muttered something inside, and she looked away.

Tallest's mount skittered closer to the coach door. 'Everyone out!' yelled Tallest. 'I want you all ...' his voice broke off.

Something was wrong. Something was very wrong. Even Fred could sense it now. I could feel him tense up on my back. The driver was too obliging; the passengers not scared enough. Hoof beats rang out suddenly, round the bend ...

'A trap!' yelled Tallest. 'Troopers! Run for it, boys!'

They were gone before I had time to blink. The chest rolled onto the ground. Fred's spurs pressed into my sides, but I'd leapt before I felt them.

Something barked behind me — a new smell, harsh and sour. One of the troopers had fired their pistol.

I half expected the bushrangers to return fire, but what would be the point? Firing pistols would slow them down. Better to gallop off to safety, out of the reach of pistol fire. Their horses were finer than anything the troopers would be riding …

Two of their horses, at any rate. Fred only had me.

I tried. I bent my head. I pushed my legs, my heart, my breath. I did the best I could. Fred knew it. I never felt the spurs again. His head bent low above me. He whispered, 'You can do it, boy.'

I couldn't. I didn't have their speed. The two other horses grew further away in front. Another pistol barked behind. I felt Fred start, then slump. They'd hit him.

I pushed myself harder than I ever had before. The horses in front were no nearer, but I heard the hoof beats behind me growing slowly fainter. I was leaving them behind.

Along the dusty road and round a bend, along the road again … They were no closer but still no further away behind. Another pistol shot. Was I out of reach or not?

Suddenly the horses in front swerved into the bush. There was no answering tug of the reins or words above from Fred, but at least he was still in the saddle.

I dashed from the road after them.

We were under the trees now. Instinctively I knew that Fred was too dazed to duck away from branches. I swerved, trying to keep the way as clear as possible.

Down a gully, slippery with ferns and mossy ks. I mightn't have the speed out on the road, but I knew how to scramble down a gully and up the other side. The hoof beats behind were fainter now; the horses in front still close enough to see.

Up into the hills, and I was gaining on them now. I was good on hills in those days. Up and up and further up, out of the valley and along the ridge our hooves striking at the stones, then down the other side where trees grew thick again and wattle dusted from overhead. Another gully and thicker trees.

There was no pressure on my reins at all now. Fred sat limply in the saddle, his upper body lying along my neck, but at least he was still there.

The moon had set. The evening star had faded. The yellow stars whitened and lost their fire. The sky turned pink, and then the world turned grey instead of black. A magpie called somewhere, and then a kookaburra. The trees looked broken against the paler sky.

There was no sound of pursuit now. But the troopers might be doubling round; they might catch us still. The bushrangers' horses galloped through the trees, and I still followed.

The ground levelled out. Thin soil and thinner trees and gleams of quartz that caught the sun. No wombat holes at least: the country was too poor for wombats here.

Still we kept on running.

The sun climbed harsh and hot above the trees. The sweat ran down my legs; my back screamed under the saddle. I'd never been ridden so fast, so hot, so long. Fred slumped across my neck. I kept my galloping as steady as I could, for fear he might fall off.

Suddenly a fence loomed up before me. The other horses leapt it. I knew that if I tried that Fred would fall, and I would fall as well most like. I'd never jumped a fence before. I swerved as gracefully as I could. I felt Fred clutch my mane. He was conscious then at least. I galloped along the fence, and then there was a gate and there were Hairy Hands and his horse before me. He swung down off his horse and pulled the gate open. 'Not long now,' he said to Fred. 'Hold hard.'

Across a paddock more stones than potatoes, then up a rise. There were fruit trees and what looked like a farm, and a tumbledown shed, and the welcome barking of dogs. I caught the smell of sheep. My breath was tearing at my lungs. I could hardly see or walk. But suddenly I heard a 'Whoa, boy, whoa.' A hand grabbed at my bridle and Fred was lifted off.

'How is he?' asked Tallest's voice and then a woman's voice asked, 'What's wrong?'

I stood there, trying to draw breath. The hot sweat dried upon my sides. I longed to drink and to shift the saddle's weight. How had I ever thought it light? Then finally there were hands tugging at my reins. I was led off to the shed. The hands lifted off my saddle and rubbed me down. I was led up and down until my ribs stopped heaving and the sweat stopped breaking through my coat. At long last there was water in a bucket. I drank and hung my head.

Someone else came into the shed. 'He did alright,' said a voice. It was Hairy Hands, who had been so scornful before.

'Who'd have thought it?' That was Tallest. He stroked my neck. 'The boy was right. He's got a heart in him, this horse has.'

'He's done for now, though,' said Hairy Hands.

'No matter,' said Tallest. 'Fred can double-back with me till we get home.' And I realised that we hadn't arrived at safety yet. 'The other horses should be right to go in an hour or so.'

'And Fred?'

'He'll have to be,' said Tallest shortly. 'We can't stop here. This place is good enough to keep dark in for an hour or two, but it won't be safe for long.'

They left me then. I looked around the shed. Bark walls, hens scratching in the straw. This might be my life when the bushrangers left, pulling a plough among the potatoes. Or, even worse, sold off to Cobb and Co.

I dozed, on and off. I was too wary to doze long. The hay smelt musty too.

Suddenly there were voices again, outside: a man's voice, a stranger, and Tallest and the woman I'd heard before. Then Hairy Hands came in and led the other horses out. He left me there.

Then there was another voice. It was Fred's. He was protesting about something. His voice was weak, but stubborn.

'No,' he said. 'You have to take him back! Not today, he's done enough today. Tomorrow. Look, here's some cash.' I heard the clink of coins. 'Five pounds. That should be enough for ten times the trouble. That horse, he saved my life. I want him taken home!'

There was a mutter, then Tallest's voice, hard and harsh. 'Look sharp! We've no time for chat! You heard what he said. And you know what you can expect if it's not done.'

Another mutter, then the sound of two fine horses, bushrangers' horses, cantering up the road.

So he took me home, the stranger from the farm, leading me by easy stages down the valley road while he rode another horse in front.

It was good to be home with the hills around me and the familiar echoes of the diggers down the road. Mrs Cooper hugged me and gave me oats, just like after I'd done the mail, and Mr Cooper brought me down an apple and treated the sores on my back that I'd got from being ridden hard for so long.

There was no sign of Centipede, that fine big chestnut horse, in our paddock. I suppose his original owners had collected him already. News of a horse like that spreads fast.

Mr Cooper took Rex with the mail the next time, to give me a rest. But they were two nights gone, not one, with Mrs Cooper looking anxiously through the window. Rex just didn't know the route like me and besides, he'd speed for half an hour and limp the rest. He never learnt to pace himself, old Rex.

So things returned to normal, or almost so.

For years I listened on moonlit nights, in case the clip of hooves came down the road again. But all I heard were possums in the trees and the wombat grunting and Mrs Cooper's snores that floated out the window till Mr Cooper nudged her to roll over and then the house was quiet.

For years I wondered what had happened to Fred. Did he recover from his wound? Did he keep at bushranging till they caught him and hung him by the neck till he was dead?

When people passed, I listened to their voices to see if I could pick Fred's out. More people came to the post office now. They built a bank down the road too, and a police station and then a courthouse, as well. The telegraph line arrived at the post office. The Coopers now cashed money orders. Their son came to live with them, bringing his wife, to help deliver the telegrams across the valley.

Sometimes when the coach dropped off the mail, there'd be a crowd of people gossiping on the post office steps: the children with their lollipops, the women in their go-to-town hats, the men discussing cattle prices or how much gold the White Ridge mine was crushing.

It was on a day like this — an ordinary sort of day — that one of the men strolled down towards our paddock. He had a beard and wore boots and moleskins like any of the farmers on the steps. He clicked his fingers at me and held something in his hand.

I wandered over, and he held it out. It was a carrot.

I took it from his hand and crunched it between my teeth, and the same hand stroked my neck. 'Thanks, Patches,' was all he said. Then he was gone.

No bushranger dies old. I like to think that night taught Fred a lesson, just like it taught me.

You know, I'd dreamt before that day: dreamt I was a brumby like my father, with a harem of mares hidden in the bush. Dreamt I was a racehorse, winning the Hawkesbury Guineas by six lengths. Dreamt I galloped with a bushranger, down a moonlit road.

And now? I stand in my paddock with Sam and Rex. We chase the roos who trespass on our grass, ignore the wombats as they chomp the tussocks or scratch inside their holes.

I feel the sunlight on my back or the rain that brings the grass and eat my oats twice each fortnight, when we leave with the mail bags and when we return, and I glance at Mr Cooper through the window munching at his buttered scones while Mrs Cooper stokes the fire up in the stove.

They're small pleasures compared to the wild ride I knew that night. But I am content.

I hope that somehow Fred has learnt those pleasures too: the gentle joy of tending a corn crop by the creek or watching his children play among the trees. Maybe he has even learnt to enjoy riding a horse like me, a steady loyal horse, who was never meant to carry a bushranger, but was a king, for a short time, in the night.

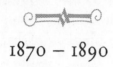

## 1870 – 1890

Bushrangers roamed the hills all through the late nineteen hundreds, but as the gold rush began to fade, farming took over (though there were still mines along the valley) and after 1861 the Land Selections Acts meant that poorer farmers could buy land and pay back the cost gradually.

But most of the good land had already been taken up by earlier landowners, who rented out claims to the gold miners. Up on the tableland the large landowners selected many plots of land in the names of their servants and their holdings grew even larger, while they grew rich from wool sold to make uniforms for wars overseas.

Down in the valley, however, there were few really large landowners. Most farmers kept cattle, not the sheep that made the graziers rich.

Even during the gold rush cattle had grazed on the hills, kept from straying too far by cliffs and gorges. Cattle were too large for dingoes to drag down, unlike the sheep that needed shepherds to guard them up on the tablelands. But cattle prices were low, especially as kerosene was now used for lighting instead of tallow candles made from boiled down cattle fat.

Most of the small farmers in the valley also worked in the mines to get enough money to live on, crushing rock with giant machines to get the gold out. Some farmers worked for wages on one of the large claims that had giant sluicers that washed out the gold.

Most households grew or made just about everything they used: they made rugs from home-tanned rabbit skins, and they made their own soap, candles and collected their own honey, and grew vegetables like potatoes, corn and turnips. They only bought things like flour, sugar, salt, tea, baking powder, dried fruit or cocoa, which was stored in big brown or cream crocks in the storeroom or larder, or at the back of the kitchen away from the stove.

For the first time since humans came to the valley, there were now rich and poor people in the district. The rich included bank managers and mill owners and large landowners who had servants and stone houses, where the women played the piano and wore corsets so tight they had no choice other than to be ladylike, with small steps and soft voices. Poor people's land was rocky and far from water, and the women's lives involved work as heavy and dirty as that done by most men.

But at least most white people could own or lease some sort of land if they wanted it.

There were those who no longer had a land at all.

## 1900

# MAGGIE

Every Monday Mama took Louisa shopping — to the dressmaker's, perhaps, for a fitting for a new dress, or to the milliner's or the haberdashery for gloves. Shopping meant tea and scones or rock cakes thick with currants and, afterwards, a walk along the main street up to the cordial factory to leave their weekly order.

To get to the cordial factory you had to walk past the saddlery and harness-maker's, the tannery and curriery, past Johnstone the Undertakers with the coffin in the window, the dispensary, the butcher's with the sheep's head on a plate, the provision store with its barrels of butter, giant cheeses and slabs of bacon.

It was a good solid town now: a town built by gold, gold from down the valley, gold from the other mining villages around. The gold was deposited in Papa's bank and the bank lent the money to build solid two-storey granite buildings.

'If it wasn't for men like me,' Papa once said, 'this place wouldn't exist.' And he'd explained how men like him had turned a wilderness into farms and roads, and a shanty town of mud and grog shops into a civilised community with shops and a library and fine buildings. The grandest building of all was the courthouse, with its tall pillars and marble stairs.

Court was in session today, Louisa noticed, peering in over the hatted women and men with neatly oiled hair. For once the wide doors were open. Someone must have just gone in and forgotten to shut them.

'Louisa! Don't stare!' Mama's gloved hand pulled Louisa's.

'I wasn't...' began Louisa, staring even harder. She'd never seen inside the courthouse before. She could just hear the magistrate intoning, '... drunk and disorderly. I hereby sentence you ...'

Mama pulled her past the door, her silk skirts swishing indignantly.

'It's not nice to stare. Ladies don't ...'

Someone screamed inside the courthouse. Louisa had never heard a scream like that before. Even the dogs were shocked to silence. The horses stopped in the street. The pigeons scratching in the horse droppings lifted their heads.

A woman burst from the courthouse. Her skin was black, her dress was ragged at the hem. Her hair was grey and wild. She was still screaming.

'Louisa! Come away!'

'But Mama ... what's happening?'

The woman ran down the footpath. It was as though she didn't see the women in their gloves and

hats and shawls or the dogs investigating the lamp posts. She simply ran and they made way for her, the women staring, small boys laughing as she ran, the dogs barking as they ran alongside.

The crowd was spilling down the courthouse stairs, gazing down the street at the running woman. Louisa heard the words 'Old Maggie'.

Mama tugged Louisa's hand. 'You don't want to see things like that! It's not right, having a woman like that right here in town. You'd think we were back in the gold rush days!'

'But, Mama! What's wrong with her? Why is she screaming?'

'Hush!' said Mama. 'There are some things young ladies don't need to know about.'

They turned the corner to the cordial factory. The sounds of the main street — the laughter, the whinnying horses, the screams — faded. The air here seemed sticky and thick with the smells of simmering cherries and pears and ginger.

'A case of cherry cider,' ordered Mama. 'And one of sarsparilla and one of ginger beer. To be delivered. You have the address? Thank you.'

She put up her sunshade as she came out. Mama was always careful not to let the sun coarsen her skin. A group of girls ran past, barefoot and laughing. School must be out, thought Louisa. She'd have liked to go to school, but Mama wouldn't let her mix with barefoot kids. Mama could teach her all she needed to know, with art lessons from Miss Harringdon and piano lessons from Mr Fletcher on Saturday afternoons.

They turned the corner back into the main street. The crowd had vanished from the courthouse steps.

But the screams still echoed up the hill.

~

Breakfast was at half past eight each morning, early enough to allow Papa to open the bank at ten o'clock, late enough to let Mama spend the necessary hour twisting Louisa's hair into ringlets with the hot crimping iron and padding out her own with false chignons, and getting Marjory the parlour maid to 'put the knee in' and pull her corset strings to the necessary tightness.

Papa was at the big dark breakfast table when Louisa and Mama went in, his plate of porridge in front of him.

'Good morning, Papa.' Louisa dutifully kissed his cheek. He smelt of hair oil and bay rum and his wool suit smelt of sweat.

'Good morning, my dear.' Papa put the newspaper down on the polished table. 'Did you sleep well?'

'Quite well, thank you, Papa.' Louisa sat down in front of her bowl of porridge, then reached for the silver jug and began to pour cream carefully around the edges.

Papa frowned. 'My dear, ring for Marjory, will you? This toast's like leather.'

Mama leant over and pulled the long bell pull. No one answered.

Mama sighed. 'Gossiping with the milk boy probably. Louisa, would you go and ask for fresh toast, please?'

'Yes, Mama.'

Louisa put her napkin back on the table and walked down the hallway to the kitchen. She pushed open the door.

Marjory and Cook were at the back door and there was the milk boy, just as Mama had expected, their billy of fresh milk in his hand.

'Dead as a doornail,' he was saying, 'just lying there she was. She ran all the way from town screaming and screaming, then just dropped dead, right there, looking out on the valley.'

'Well, at least she saw it again before she died,' said Cook comfortably.

'Please,' said Louisa. 'Mama said could we have fresh toast?'

The milk boy started and touched his cap to her.

'Certainly, Miss Louisa,' said Cook. 'Will that be all?'

'Yes, thank you,' said Louisa. She paused. 'That person you were talking about — was that the old black woman from the courthouse?'

'Old Maggie,' said the milk boy. He was about her age. He had bare feet and his cap was stained and greasy. 'She was a right one, they say. Escaped being rounded up with the other blacks somehow. Lived all her life down in the valley. Used to make a devil of a fuss when she'd got some rum in her. The Valley Ladies' Guild, they told the police to get rid of her.'

'I saw her,' said Louisa softly. 'I heard her screaming.'

The boy met her eyes. 'Broke her heart, I reckon, that magistrate saying they'd lock her up then send her to the camp down the coast.'

A broken heart, thought Louisa. That's what that scream sounded like. The sound of a heart breaking. Imagine loving a place so much it broke your heart to leave it. For a moment her life felt empty.

'Time you were off,' Cook said firmly to the milk boy. She took the billy of milk and shut the door and turned to Louisa. 'I'll bring the toast in a minute, Miss.'

'Thank you,' said Louisa.

She pushed through the swinging door out into the dark wooden hall, which smelt of floor polish and pot pourri and Mama's gardenia scent.

The carpet was soft under her boots, the starched ruffles rustled on her dress. But she could still hear the screams.

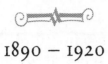

# 1890 – 1920

When white settlers first came to the valley, the valley's Aboriginal people were generally taller, stronger, faster and more muscular than the new settlers. In those days the valley was an almost paradise where you could make little affort to live well.

Although there were none of the massacres or poisoning of Aborigines here that happened in other areas, within a few decades most of them had died of measles or flu or smallpox or tuberculosis, or of starvation as their land was taken for mining or farming. Many were killed, or forced down to the coast in battles with Aboriginal men from much further away, who had also had their land taken from them, and some were sent to the camps at the coast by local magistrates.

By 1890 the few remaining Aboriginal people worked either as servants or farm hands, usually just for food and clothing. Their employers didn't given them the wages that white workers received in case they put it to 'improper use'. Their Aboriginal names had been changed to insulting nicknames: Curraralt became 'Frying Pan Jack', Winbirrba became 'Dirty Dick', Nollawarra 'Stupid Tommy', Bobbingall 'Billy the Bull' and Currningnang was 'Crankie'.

Those who didn't choose to spend their lives as unpaid servants to white masters hunted where they could, begged for food or alcohol, or sold the only thing the new settlers would pay for — their bodies.

The valley was very different from the quiet world of waterlily feasts and wild ducks they'd known, and now it would change again.

Now the dredges had come to the valley — great wood-powered machines that sifted the sand and mud and gravel faster than human hands could manage and ate up all the trees that could be hauled for them. The hills were bare except for stumps and grass and brown smudges, as the land washed away without the trees to hold the topsoil in place.

The air smelt of smoke and the cold smell of crushed rock from the few remaining mines (most mines now filled with water before the miners reached gold-bearing rock), and the lagoons where the dredges dug stank of stagnant water and sewerage.

The only tall trees now clung among the cliffs and up in the gorge country where it was too steep to fell them and roll them down to the flat land and the waiting dredges.

In nineteen fourteen war came to the world outside the valley. Many of the valley's young men volunteered to fight for the English 'motherland' few of them had ever seen — and that would do little, if anything, for them in return.

Churches, schools and newspapers thundered about the brutishness and frightfulness of the German 'Huns' (the enemy in every war is always seen as brutish and frightful). Women made jam, and 'Anzac' biscuits to raise money for the soldiers, and knitted socks and scarves and balaclavas to send to them in battle.

Most of the young men who sailed away to war never returned. Those who did come back rarely spoke of the horror they had seen in the trenches.

Many of the valley's mines closed down during the war, as there were no longer enough men to work them. Only one dredge worked full time, as wages were higher now that labour was scarce, and the cost of firewood to run the dredges was higher too. But one hundred men were still employed in dredging, even during nineteen nineteen when more people died worldwide from flu than in the war.

But by the end of the 'war to end all wars' (at the beginning of every war people think that fighting will solve all problems, instead of creating new ones) most of the valley's gold had already been mined, and by nineteen twenty even the power of the dredges could no longer find much gold.

# 1922

## ALICE AND THE YOWIE

'Hey, Sis! They're shutting down the dredge!' George climbed up on the water barrel by the laundry tub and bit into his apple. It had grown wrinkled through the winter but was still sweet.

Ellen lifted Brownie the wombat out of the copper (he liked to chew the edges), poured in a bucket of water and held a match to the twigs and crumpled paper under the copper to light the fire to heat the washing water.

'They've been talking about closing the dredge down for years. No, stop it, you stupid animal! Wombats don't eat soap.' She shoved the cockatoo off the scrubbing brush and began to rub at the gravy stain on Alice's vest. 'Could you split some more wood, love? We're almost out of kindling.'

'But this time they're really going to! Mr Dillon at the butcher's shop told me!'

'What were you doing at the butcher's?'

'Helping unload the rabbits. Mr Dillon gave me a penny *and* two rabbits.'

'I don't want you accepting charity,' began Ellen,

then stopped. Since Pa had died, the only money coming in had been what Will earnt cutting the timber for the dredge's engines and the little she got for doing the Andersons' washing. Every penny was precious. And if the dredge really was going to shut down ...

'It wasn't charity! I worked for it! I put the rabbits in the meat safe,' added George.

'Thanks, love. I'm sorry I was crotchety. No, stop it!' she added to Brownie the wombat. 'George, take that boot away from him will you? He'll chew a hole in a minute.'

'Cockie want an apple!' screamed Mr Feathers from his perch on the mangle.

George slipped down from the barrel and put the boots up on the shelf, along with the doormat and the rag rug and all the other things that wombats liked to chew.

Ellen was always taking in injured animals. Mr Feathers had been found with a broken wing up by the logging camp. He still couldn't fly though he hopped happily from sofa to table to meat safe. Brownie's mum had been killed by dogs and Grunty the koala had been crushed when his tree was felled.

No one had thought Grunty would survive, but ever since Mum and Millie had died in the influenza epidemic, and Dad had drowned when the Number Two dredge sank, it was as though Ellen was determined to cheat death of any other victims.

Or maybe, thought George, tossing the apple core down to Brownie, she just liked looking after things.

Ellen let the vest slide back to soak into the washing tub and inspected one of Will's shirts for stains. 'Where's Alice?'

'She went off with the other girls after school to see Betty Carter's kittens.'

'But they're all older than her! They can't want a little 'un tagging along with them.'

George shrugged. Alice did what Alice wanted to. 'Can I have some bread and plum jam when I've got the wood?'

'Finish the melon jam before you start the plum.'

'But I hate melon ...'

'Ellen? Ellen where are you?'

'In the laundry!' called Ellen.

Mrs Carter's skirts rustled as she hurried around the house. All the younger women in the valley wore short skirts almost up to their knees now — some had even had their hair cut short too — but Mrs Carter said she'd die of shame if any man saw her lower limbs. 'Oh, Ellen ...' she stopped, as though trying to work out how to break the news.

Ellen's face froze the way it had when they'd seen the dredge slowly turn over in the muddy lagoon and known that Dad was in the engine room. 'It's not ... it's not Will?' Axes could slip and slice you open; trees could fall the wrong way.

'No, not Will. Is ... is Alice here?' There was a faint hope in Mrs Carter's voice.

'No! George said she was with the other girls. Please, what's happened?'

'The girls went up the gully to look for raspberries, then one of them noticed she wasn't there. She must have wandered off all by herself! They called and called then Betty ran back to tell me. The girls have asked everywhere but no one's seen her. Oh, my dear, I'm so sorry!'

~

You could hear the echo of the searchers' cooees and see their lanterns from the window — tiny yellow glows weaving across the hills then disappearing as the men dropped into gullies or climbed high up to the ridges where there were still trees. All the lower hills along the valley were bare of trees now: dredge engines were hungry beasts and needed load after load of wood to keep on firing.

Something really bad must have happened for anyone to get lost up there, thought George desperately. Especially Alice! Alice was only five but she always knew exactly what she was doing.

Maybe she fell down an abandoned mine. Maybe she'd tried to swim in the dredge holes and drowned in the cold stagnant water. Maybe a snake bit her.

It's not fair, he thought. We've already lost so much. We can't lose Alice too! Alice is a pest, but she's *our* pest.

Will was up there searching too. The house was quiet. George had never known it as quiet as this. Maybe it's quiet when we're at school and Will's at work, thought George, and Ellen's here by herself.

Mrs Carter had brought a pot of Irish stew. It was what you did when tragedy struck the valley — you brought food. Ellen had shoved it to the back of the stove to keep warm. Neither of them felt like eating.

'Cockie wants a plum cake!' yelled Mr Feathers, shattering the silence. George and Ellen ignored him.

'She'll be alright,' said George, for what must have been the hundredth time.

'Of course she will,' said Ellen. She hadn't touched the tea she had brewed for both of them.

She's trying to comfort me and I'm trying to comfort her, thought George. We're lying to each other.

'Why hasn't she heard them calling?' cried Ellen. 'Why won't she answer?'

Because she's unconscious down a mine hole, thought George. But instead he said, 'Maybe she's fallen asleep.'

Ellen bit her lip. 'If only we could do something! If only ...'

'Ellie? Ellie, I'm tired!'

Ellen sprang to her feet. 'Alice!'

Alice stumbled into the lamplight. Ellen rushed towards her and gathered her up. 'What happened? Where have you been all this time? You naughty girl! Are you alright? You're not hurt?' Her voice wobbled between anger and sobs.

'I'm alright,' said Alice. 'Can I have some cocoa?'

'But where were you?' cried Ellen

'I was with the yowie,' said Alice.

⁓

George ran to ring the church bell to call the searchers back, then raced back home. Alice was sitting among the cushions in Dad's old armchair and sucking her thumb, with Brownie stretched out on her lap, chewing a carrot, and Ellen crouched down in front of her.

Ellen pulled Alice's thumb out gently. 'You can't talk and suck your thumb,' she said. 'What happened, Alice?'

Alice considered. 'It was the flutterby,' she said at last.

'She means butterfly,' said George.

Alice nodded. 'It was a big brown one. I ran after it and it wouldn't stop. An' then I falled down. It was a hole.'

Ellen's face went even whiter. 'A mine shaft,' she whispered.

'An' I cried and then the yowie came. Can I have cocoa, please Ellie? With four sugars?'

'Two sugars,' said Ellen automatically.

'Four,' said Alice.

'Three then. George, would you put it on?' asked Ellen.

George ran out into the larder and grabbed the jug of milk from its shelf. The cream had risen to the top during the day and formed a thin yellow crust on top. He pushed it away with the back of a spoon and poured the milk into a pan, then stirred the cocoa powder and sugar into it and put the pan on the stove. Ellen had banked the fire down for the night, but the brown milk still frothed up almost at once. He poured it into a cup and handed it to Alice.

Alice sipped it calmly, as though she'd done nothing more scary than do pot hooks all day at school.

'Say thank you to George,' said Ellen.

'Thank you, George,' said Alice without looking at him.

Ellen took a deep breath. 'Alice, what *really* happened? I won't be cross, I promise.'

'I *said* what happened.' Alice sounded slightly annoyed. 'The yowie came.'

'Alice there are no such things as yowies!'

'Yes there are,' said Alice matter-of-factly. 'Mrs Ferguson said a Gooligah scared her grandma when she was just a little girl, but Betty Carter says it was really a yowie.'

'You're telling porkies!' accused George.

'No, I'm not,' said Alice, calmly taking another sip of cocoa.

'Yes, you are,' began George, but Ellen shook her head at him. She pulled out her hanky and wiped off Alice's cocoa moustache. 'Tell us about the yowie, Alice.'

'He was big and hairy,' said Alice. 'That's how I knowed it was a yowie. And his face was all scrunched up, like this.' She flattened her nose with her hand. 'He leant down and pulled me out of the hole and ...'

'Did he wear any clothes?' asked George.

'It's rude to have no clothes on. He had pants,' said Alice. 'But all the rest of him was hairy. His face and arms and legs and ...' she indicated her chest, 'an' ... an' everything. His hair was longer than mine! But nobody had plaited it,' she added.

'What happened then?' asked Ellen quietly.

'He tooked me to his cave 'cause I had a cut. See?'
She pointed to a long thin scratch on her arm. 'And
my legs was dirty too,' she added. Alice hated to be
dirty.

'You might have drowned down there,' Ellen
stopped and shivered. Most of the abandoned mines
were half full of water.

'There aren't any caves in the valley!' protested
George.

'There was so too,' said Alice stubbornly. 'An'
...an' he had golden elephants all along a shelf an' ...'

'Golden elephants!' exclaimed George.

'An' he washed my cut and I washed my legs an'
then we had dinner.' She yawned. 'Ellie, I'm tired!'

'I suppose he gave you roast goose,' said George
scornfully.

'No, silly. Yowies don't eat roast goose.'

'You're just stupid,' announced George.

'You're stupid too, then,' said Alice. 'Yowies eat
eggs an' nuts an' oranges. It wasn't a very good
dinner,' she added sleepily. 'Then I was tired so I said
he had to take me home.'

'What did the yowie say to that?' demanded
George.

'He said he couldn't take me down here because
there were guns and things. But I said I was too tired
to walk so he had to carry me. And then he said
alright.'

George snorted. Sooner or later Alice managed to
get what she wanted from everyone — even imaginary
yowies, apparently.

'Then he carried me on his shoulders till I could see the houses and the lights and then he said, "Run home now," 'cause he couldn't come closer because the men shoot yowies.' She frowned, half asleep. 'No one will shoot my yowie will they? He's nice.'

'No one will shoot your yowie,' said Ellen soothingly.

'He's a really nice yowie,' Alice's eyes were drooping. 'You'd really like my yowie, Ellen.'

'Come on,' said Ellen gently. 'It's bedtime now.'

'Carry me?' asked Alice.

Ellen lifted her up. 'Time you went to bed, too,' she said to George.

⌒

The sheets were cold in the bed in the sleepout he shared with Will. George pulled the comforter up to his chin and listened to the dingoes howl up on the ridges. Then he heard the bang of the back door and Will's weary voice as he helped himself to the stew; the thumps as Ellen kneaded the dough so it could rise during the night and they'd have fresh bread at breakfast; the sounds of Brownie gnawing the table leg and Mr Feathers chortling 'Hello Cockie' happily to himself.

'Will?' Ellen said.

'Mmm?' Will's mouth sounded full of bread and stew.

'What do you think really happened?'

'I don't know. All that about a cave and golden elephants ... there's nothing like a cave in the valley. Or golden elephants. Or a yowie either,' he added tiredly.

97

'Maybe she fell asleep and dreamt it all. But why didn't she hear everyone calling? And how did she get back in the dark?'

'Maybe it was a sound sleep and she was behind a rock or something. Maybe she hit her head and was knocked out.'

'But there's no sign of a bruise! She's not even dirty!'

George could hear Will's sigh. 'Alice is never dirty! She won't let dirt stick to her. She just gives it one of her looks ... Look, let's leave it, alright? I've been out there all bally night and so has every other bloke in the valley. She's safe now. That's what matters.'

'Yes,' said Ellen slowly. 'She's safe now. Will, George said they're going to shut the dredge down.'

'Yes,' said Will flatly. 'They paid us off today. The company only got four hundred ounces last year. There's just not enough gold left to make it worthwhile.'

'But what will we do?'

Will shrugged. 'Get another job somehow — Eucy cutting or I'll see if they want someone down at the cheese factory.'

'Everyone else will be looking for jobs too.'

'If the worst comes to the worst, I'll go rabbit trapping. There's still a bit of money in bunnies.' He sighed. 'Sis, do you ever think what we'd be doing now if Mum and Dad hadn't died?'

'No,' said Ellen tightly.

'Bloke up on the tableland, he's started a garage. Says there's going to be more and more cars around soon. Strewth, I'd like to be part of that.' There was silence, then Will added awkwardly, 'Don't cry, Sis. Please don't cry.'

'It's my fault! If I'd been looking after her properly, she wouldn't have got lost!'

'She's not lost. She's safe back home. We'll be right, Sis. We've managed up till now.'

'Yes,' said Ellen. 'We've managed.' But her voice was unimaginably tired.

<hr>

Will left early next morning to walk to the cheese factory and see if they were taking on more hands. 'Might see if Fergusons want some fencing done too,' he said to George, as he buckled the snakeskin belt he'd inherited from Dad.

George waited till he smelt the bread in the oven before he got up. He pulled on shirt and trousers quickly (they were old ones of Dad's cut down to fit him; but he still needed braces to keep the trousers up) and wandered into the kitchen.

Ellen looked up from scrubbing the kitchen table. 'Washed your face?'

'Yep.'

She inspected him. 'You've still got sleep in your eyes.'

'Aw, Ellen …'

'Wash!'

George straggled out through the sleepout again and out the door to the water trough. The grass was cold on his bare feet, though not as freezing as it was in winter. Then the only way to thaw them was to warm them in hot, fresh horse droppings, or cattle manure down at the dairy.

Alice was sitting at the kitchen table when he came in. Ellen slid their plates across the table; the scrambled eggs were soaking into the big slabs of bread toasted by the stove's firebox.

'Mrs Carter's eggs,' said Ellen. 'Her hens are laying more than they can eat.'

And Mrs Carter had been Mum's best friend, thought George, and she's going to make sure none of Mum's kids go hungry. But he didn't say anything.

Alice took a bite of her eggs. 'Can my yowie come to breakfast one day?' she asked. 'Yowies don't get scrambled eggs for breakfast.'

'I thought you said the yowie wouldn't come down here in case someone shoots him,' said George.

'Don't talk with your mouth full,' said Ellen tiredly.

'Cockie want a biscuit!' yelled Mr Feathers.

'My yowie really needs someone to make him breakfast,' said Alice, carefully cutting off her crusts and pushing them to the side of the plate.

'Crusts make your hair curly,' said George.

'I don't want curly hair,' said Alice. Mr Feathers jumped onto the back of her chair and she passed him a crust. 'Please can my Yowie come to breakfast one day, Ellen?'

'Alice, stop talking about the yowie,' said Ellen wearily. There were purple shadows, like thunderclouds, under her eyes. 'You know it isn't true!'

'Yes, it is! You'd like my yowie! You have to ask my Yowie to breakfast 'cause ...'

Ellen shut her eyes briefly then opened them again. 'No more yowies! You'll be late.' She handed them each a packet of sandwiches and an apple, wrapped up in much creased brown paper. She hesitated. 'Alice, promise you'll come straight home from school today. Promise!'

'I promise,' said Alice readily.

'And George ... you'll stay with her all the way to school and see she gets home safely? Promise too?'

'Course,' said George, affronted. Surely Ellen knew she could trust him. He shouldn't have to promise.

Ellen still looked worried. 'I'd come with you but I've got all that washing to do for Mrs Anderson.'

The Andersons were one of the big landowners in the valley. They'd made their money selling mutton to the miners and renting land to them at twenty shillings a plot, and now the gold was almost gone, they were making almost as much money sending their milk to the cheese factory.

It was funny to think that maybe one day everyone in the valley would be breeding cows or horses or growing vegetables, thought George, and no one would be looking for gold at all.

He pushed his chair back and grabbed his sandwiches. 'Come on,' he said to Alice. 'The bell will go before we get there if we don't watch out.'

～

There was only one main street in the valley now. Their house was at one end and the school was at the other. In between them were the town's remaining pub and the butcher's shop and Ah Ping's general store and the three churches and a handful of houses, separated by paddocks with horses and thistles and Jersey cows slowly munching grass, as they watched the humans pass.

Once streets and tracks had led all over the valley. Now the grass had grown over most of them. The wattle and daub huts were slowly collapsing into the soil, with only their crumbling chimneys to show where they had been.

Above the main street the bare hills crowded one after the other till they met the blue-treed ridges, even bluer now in the thin haze of dredge smoke. Below, the thistles grew on mounds of sand and mullock heaps that the floods covered when it rained, with the deep stinking dredge holes the only signs of the bright clear river that had once flowed through the valley.

It must have been weird to have been here when the whole valley crawled with people, thought George. Forty thousand people — he couldn't even imagine so many now. And trees everywhere too, and kangaroos.

Alice trudged beside him. Suddenly she stopped.

'What's up?'

'I want to see my yowie.'

'Look, to heck with your bally yowie!'

'Ellen says no swearing,' said Alice calmly.

'Well, she says no telling lies too!'

'I don't tell lies,' stated Alice.

George was silent. It was true, he thought. Alice didn't tell lies. She might be ten dozen types of pest, but she didn't tell lies. And if Alice didn't tell lies...

'Alice,' he said carefully. 'Did you really see a yowie?'

'Of course,' said Alice. 'I said I did, didn't I?'

'I mean ... I mean are you *sure* it was a yowie?'

Alice looked at him scornfully. 'Yes!'

'And he really had gold elephants in his cave?'

'I *told* you he did.' Alice turned suddenly and began to stomp up one of the old grassy tracks on the hill.

George ran after her. 'Where are you going?'

'I *told* you — to see my yowie.'

'But you got lost! You don't know the way!'

'Yes, I do,' said Alice impatiently. 'I got lost and *then* I went to the yowie's cave and *then* he took me home. I don't know where I got lost but I know where my yowie is.'

'Then why didn't you tell Ellen?'

''Cause she didn't ask me,' said Alice, as though it were obvious. She marched a little faster, her long skirt protecting her short legs from the thistles.

'Hey, wait up! You promised Ellen you'd go straight to school!' said George.

'No, I didn't! I promised I'd come straight *home* from school.' Alice kept on trudging.

'But ...' George scrambled after her. Maybe ... maybe there really was a yowie and a yowie's cave and golden elephants ...

No, there couldn't be golden elephants. But maybe ... maybe they were great big nuggets that *looked* like elephants, like that nugget they called the Old Potato and the one that looked just like a horse and rider. George imagined lugging a great nugget home to Ellen. Then they'd be rich and she wouldn't have to do Mrs Anderson's washing and ...

No. It was impossible! There was no yowie and no golden elephants.

'Someone'll see us!' said George. 'They'll tell Ellen you've wagged school and then you'll really get it!'

Alice shrugged and pushed past a tall thistle, almost as high as her head.

'She'll...' George stopped. Ellen threatened spankings but she'd never spanked anyone, not even when he'd tried to sail the wash tub in the dredge hole and it had sunk and he'd nearly drowned. When Ellen found out that Alice hadn't gone to school, she wouldn't even be angry, George realised. She'd just be upset and feel she'd failed them again and cry when she thought they couldn't hear her.

He stopped. 'You can't do this to Ellen,' he said. 'It's not fair!'

Alice kept on thumping through the thistles.

'She tries so hard for us!'

Alice paid no attention.

'Alice, please!' It felt all wrong having to plead with your little sister. But he couldn't very well lift her off her feet and carry her back by force.

Alice ignored him.

Well, thought George, he could try. He ran forward in a sort of crouch, like he'd seen the men do when they had to pick up a bag of potatoes and run with it at the New Year's Day Sports. His shoulder hit Alice's middle. But instead of folding neatly over his shoulder so he could carry her off, she kicked him in the ankle.

'Hey! That hurt!' He tried to shove her away and pick her up at the same time. Three seconds later they were rolling over and over in the thistles and ...

'George! Alice! What the blue blazes are you doing?' Ellen stood over them panting. 'I was just heading up to Andersons' and I saw you both. Good gravy, Alice, don't you think you've caused enough trouble already?'

George stood up and tried to pick the thistles out of his skin. 'I ... I ...' Cripes, what was he going to say now? He couldn't dob on Alice, even if it *was* her fault, even if she *was* a pest of a little sister.

'I wanted to see my yowie,' said Alice matter-of-factly.

She didn't have any thistles sticking in her at all, thought George. It wasn't fair!

Alice glanced over at George. 'He tried to make me go back,' she added contemptuously.

'Well, he was right! Come on!' Ellen grabbed Alice's hand then George's. 'School! Now!'

'No,' said Alice, digging her toes into the dirt.

'Alice ... '

Suddenly Alice's expression changed. 'Please, Ellen?' she pleaded. 'I think my yowie's hurted. Sort of hurted,' she added. 'It's not fair! And he helped me and he took me home in the dark. Please, please, please, Ellen!' She gave a tiny mournful sniff.

'But,' Ellen was weakening, as she always did when Alice pleaded. And she must want to know what really happened to Alice last night too, thought George.

'Just a few more minutes then! Till we hear the school bell! If we haven't found your yowie by then, you have to promise you'll go back without arguing!'

Alice considered. Then she nodded. 'I promise,' she said. She turned and immediately began to stomp through the thistles again. Ellen and George followed her.

The path was even fainter up here. How long had it been since a cart or sulky went this way? wondered George. The only signs there had ever been a track here were the indentations in the grass. The track must have been used a lot once to make such deep ruts in the hill.

He waited for the clanging of the school bell behind him but all he could hear was the far-off mooing of cattle. Even the dredge was silent today. George wondered if he'd ever hear the chug of its engine or the clatter of its conveyer belt again.

Alice pulled open a sagging wooden gate. 'In here,' she said.

Ellen blinked. 'This is the old Lauer place,' she said slowly. 'Peter Lauer went off to the war and old Mrs Lauer tried to keep the farm going for him, but it was all too much for her, and then he didn't come back. Then she caught the influenza,' she added softly.

'This is where my yowie lives,' Alice called back to them breathlessly. She was almost running up the hill now. She reached the top and paused, just as the bell began to ring down in the valley.

Clang! Clang! Clang!

'School!' panted Ellen, catching up to her. 'You promised, Alice!'

Alice pointed to the shallow valley below them. There was a squat stone house, almost hidden by a tangled garden, and paddocks that stretched into their own hidden valley above the valley proper. 'My yowie's down there,' said Alice simply.

All at once George understood. 'She met a swaggie!' he cried. 'He must have been sheltering in the old Lauer place and ...'

'My yowie's not a swaggie!' Alice turned her wide brown eyes on Ellen. 'Please can we go down there?' she said. 'He needs us!'

Huh! thought George. She knows what works every time.

Ellen bit her lip. Then she nodded and took their hands.

The bare hills vanished as they walked down into the valley. From here all you could see were green paddocks and old fruit trees: giant pear trees, taller than the house, an old orange tree with lichened bark, a lemon tree and a whole orchard of apples, the last of their spring blossoms falling onto the grass.

More trees lined the old driveway, so overgrown and tangled you could hardly see the house, just the door gaping under the sagging veranda. It does look like a cave, thought George. It probably looked even more like a cave last night.

And maybe if there was a 'cave' there was a yowie and golden elephants ...

The tangle of the garden grew thicker as they approached the house. Wisteria vines as thick as his wrist pushed their way under the roofing iron; a solitary rose drooped from a jungle of thorns. Part of the veranda floor had rotted away and droppings from a swallow's nest stained the rest of the boards white.

No one would live here, thought George. Surely even a Yowie would mend the steps ...

'Is anyone here?' Ellen's voice quavered as they climbed the stairs, avoiding the one that had crumbled at one side.

No answer. A swallow swooped over their heads, grabbed a fly out of the air then fluttered up to its nest. Three small bare heads popped out, already yelling for the delicacy. Ellen knocked on the door. 'Hello?'

'We have to go inside,' said Alice. She blinked troubled eyes at Ellen. 'He said the guns might shoot him! He might be hurt.'

'No one could have shot him!' said George scornfully. 'We'd have heard the noise. Anyway, you said he was hurt already.'

'Sort of hurted,' said Alice. 'He might be more hurted now.'

Ellen hesitated. 'Maybe we should just see if he's alright.'

She stepped into the dimness, with Alice and George following her.

It took a moment to get used to the gloom. Spiders' webs hung thick as curtains from the windows. Dust coated the velvet sofa and matching chairs, the once polished mantelpiece and sideboard, and a glass-fronted cabinet with leather-bound books and ... a line of elephants. But they weren't gold at all, thought George, they were brass, like the gong Ah Ping the grocer had on his counter. Trust Alice not to know the difference between gold and brass!

'Down here,' said Alice. She pushed in front, down the wide hall with its faded linoleum and shabby panelled walls and into the kitchen at the far end of the house.

The others followed her. George looked around.

More cobwebs on the stove and a fine shading of orange rust. It must be years since the stove had been lit, thought George. Surely even a swaggie would light the stove!

Shelves of crockery that looked like it had stood unused for a hundred years, dust on the window above the porcelain sink. But the sink was damp, under the big iron pump. Someone had pumped water here, and not long ago. And there was food on the table — a basket of eggs — and a sack of walnuts on the floor.

Alice said yowies live on eggs and nuts, thought George. But surely ...

From the back door came the cluck of hens and the far-off possessive yell of a rooster. And then another noise: the sound of a hand pump and water splashing into a bucket, and the thud as the bucket cracked against the pump.

Someone was out there. Someone, thought George, or something … He crossed to the window and peered out.

There was a man there, filling an old wooden bucket. Despite the long hair down to his shoulders, the hairy chest and legs in the old army shorts, he knew it was a man.

Then the man turned round.

George gasped. What had once been a face was now scars, a vivid pucker of purple and red. Half the nose was gone and most of one cheek and the scars ran deep and horrible up into the scalp.

Alice ran to the back door and opened it wide. 'Yowie? I brought Ellen. I said I would.'

The yowie — man — started, instinctively drawing the long hair over his face to hide the scars. For a moment he looked like he might flee.

'Please stay!' called Alice. 'Ellen's here.'

The man watched uncertainly as Ellen walked slowly down the steps, with George behind her. 'I'm sorry,' she said gently. 'We knocked but there was no answer. I … I want to thank you for bringing Alice home last night. We were all so worried.'

'It's alright,' said the yowie. His voice sounded hoarse, as though he didn't use it often. He kept his face averted so the scarred side didn't show. He still looked like he might run away.

'I didn't know anyone lived here.'

The yowie watched Ellen come slowly closer. 'Came back in nineteen nineteen,' he muttered. 'People stare. I don't … I don't …' His voice trailed off.

'Then you're Peter Lauer?'

The yowie nodded. 'Yes.'

Ellen held out her hand slowly, just like she held out her hand to that dog that had been caught in the rabbit trap, thought George.

'I'm Ellen, Alice's sister. And this is George ...'

Rattarattaratta ratta ... The sound of the dredge engine and conveyer belt down in the valley pounded through the silence, then echoed from the cliffs. They must be going to press one last load, thought George, before they shut it down.

The yowie screamed. It was an almost animal scream, as though he really was a Yowie, not a man. 'The guns!' he cried. 'The guns!' Suddenly he ran, shoving past them through the back door and into the kitchen.

George blinked. 'He's nutty as a fruit cake!' he said.

Ellen was silent. Then she shook her head. 'It's shell shock,' she said. 'I read about it. The guns and the noise and the death in France. Sometimes the soldiers saw so much horror they couldn't leave it behind. Poor man! Every time he hears the dredge, he must think it's the guns of France again.'

'Well, he won't have to hear them for much longer,' said George practically.

'No,' said Ellen slowly. She seemed to have come to a decision. 'George, go and get some kindling. I'm going to light that stove. Then you and Alice go back home and bring up some tea and sugar and a billy of milk and bread and a pot of jam and some butter and the green ointment on the dresser — put them all in the big basket. Can you remember that?'

'Yes,' said Alice promptly. She looked ... satisfied, thought George.

Ellen hurried up the back stairs, into the kitchen. George glanced at Alice. For a moment he wanted to ask: Did you plan all of this? Did you somehow hear that there was a man here who needed help in the same way Brownie and Mr Feathers needed help? Did you even get lost on purpose?

But that was impossible. Alice was just a little child. Even Alice couldn't ...

'Ellen said to get the kindling,' Alice reminded him.

George went over to the woodpile at the side of the house. It looked like it had been untouched for years. It'll burn hot and fast now, thought George.

Behind him in the kitchen he could hear Ellen speaking soothingly, like she had to Brownie when the trappers first brought him in, as she clanged around the firebox to light the stove.

And in front of him? Suddenly he couldn't see the tangled garden. Instead the trees had been pruned back into a long graceful drive; a car chugged up it with Will at the wheel, down for the day from his garage up in town. The fences were neat and mended, the cattle were fat, and down in the orchard kids yelled — Ellen's kids and the yowie's.

And up at the house George and the yowie discussed which new bull to buy while Ellen smiled at them across the table. The yowie's scars had faded now, and the horror had disappeared from his eyes.

And Alice? She wasn't there at all, decided George with satisfaction. She was off being Prime Minister or head of the League of Nations, while he was ...

'George? Hurry up with the kindling!' called Ellen.

George grinned and went back inside.

# 1920 – 1972

The first big flood after the dredges stopped washed the sandbanks flat, and when the flood subsided a river flowed through the valley again, fast and clear and shallow.

More floods washed the channel deeper and slowly trees began to grow along its edges — not the red gums that had grown there before (the few red gums were mostly cut for fence posts anyway) but casuarina trees that once had grown only in the high gullies.

Birds dropped seeds into the disturbed soil, and trees began to grow on the bare hills again: thorn bush and black wattles first of all, then gum trees — thin saplings that slowly grew into trees so large it seemed that they had always been there.

One by one the last mines were abandoned. More people moved away. But the scars of mining remained — the 'mullock heaps' of rock, the drifts of sand, and the eroding gullies and hills that slumped in landslides of mud and clay when it rained. Even much of the once fertile valley floor was useless now. The soil had gone or was buried and only rock and sand remained.

It was a valley of farmers now. There were beef cattle up in the hills, dairy cows on the creek flats and a cheese factory that won prizes as far away as

London with a cheddar cheese a deeper gold than the few specks that still glinted in the sand. Paddocks were ploughed for pumpkins, tomatoes, beans and passionfruit vines, and the produce was sold in the towns nearby.

Orchards began to spread slowly through the valley, slowly as people learnt what flourished — peach trees on the hills at first where the frost wasn't so severe, then when those first peach trees survived more were planted down on the creek flats. (It is said that the first peach tree was grown from a stone a tourist had thrown away.) Water was brought to dry hills by the old Chinese mining races that still crossed the valley, and pumps began to lift water from the river to the crops.

For a little while during the Depression in the nineteen thirties unemployed people came to the valley, and fossickers lined the riverbanks again and lived in shanties made of kerosene tins banged flat, with bark roofs, made just as in the early days.

One person in three in Australia was unemployed in the Depression, and the government paid one pound a week to gold prospectors. But when jobs became plentiful during World War II the prospectors left again for the army or the jobs that the war had brought that men had left as they joined up.

Their shanties fell down one by one and the big bushfire of nineteen thirty-nine burnt out the rest. Trees and thorn bush grew over the ruins, and twenty years later you couldn't see where the shanty town had been.

Radio came to the valley in the nineteen thirties and suddenly the valley's entertainment came mostly from outside, instead of songs around the piano and concert parties.

By the nineteen fifties most homes had cars. Once life in the valley had been bounded by the ridges and the valley gave its inhabitants shelter and food and friends. But now, one by one, the shops in the valley closed, as people drove to towns further away to buy their clothes and furniture and groceries.

The school closed down in the nineteen seventies. Kids had to leave home early in the morning now to catch a bus to the next town. The last shop closed, then the police station, and the post office. It was a different valley now. Wattles grew on the once bare hills; dairy cows grazed on the rocky, sandy flats where once the dredges had searched for gold, and slowly peach and apple orchards spread on the bits of good land that the dredges hadn't destroyed.

The nineteen sixties brought a drought and a government scheme to 'rationalise' the dairy industry into a few main areas. All over the state dairies and cheese factories shut down as they couldn't get a licence to operate. Australia lost most of its finest cheeses; townspeople no longer got fresh local milk, and the valley lost its cheese factory and most of its dairy cows too.

Now the farmers grazed beef cattle on the hills and along the creek instead. More and more orchards lined the valley, with the paddocks of pumpkins and beans and tomatoes.

The valley slowly slipped into a seasonal routine: pruning, planting and fencing in winter and in summer the men picked peaches and the women packed them and picked beans or capsicums or tomatoes, too. Trucks took the boxes of peaches to the city markets and small stalls lined the road selling peaches and peach jam and chutney, and maybe tomatoes and onions, to passersby.

Land was cheap in the valley now; most of the valley children left to find work elsewhere.

Then, as throughout the valley's history, new settlers came. These settlers wore cheesecloth and beads or beards. Like the settlers a hundred years before, they dreamt of owning their own land and building their own houses and growing their own food, and for a while they were very different from the other inhabitants of the valley.

## 1972

# TRUE GOLD

The school bus was winding down the road above the commune at the far end of the valley when Ellen saw the dinosaur.

It was standing on a rock. It was mottled grey and yellow, and as long as she was, with legs as thick as trunks, and a long neck with a surprisingly small head and tiny reptile eyes. Was it sleeping? No, its eyes were open. Maybe it was hunting for ... what did dinosaurs eat? wondered Ellen. She nudged Shiloh urgently 'Look, there it is again!'

'What?'

'The dinosaur!'

Shiloh turned, but the bus had gone round the next corner. 'I didn't see anything.'

'It was there — really. Just like yesterday.'

'You've got dinosaurs on the brain. There aren't any dinosaurs in the valley. There aren't any dinosaurs *anywhere*,' he said.

'But...' Ellen was going to say that maybe some dinosaurs had survived in the high steep cliffs of the valley, where it was too steep to build or farm, but

Shiloh was right. If there were still dinosaurs here, someone would have seen them.

But *she* had! Today and yesterday ...

The bus bumped across the bridge. Ellen gazed out at the paddocks of sleepy cows, the rows of peach trees, without really seeing them till the bus drew up at the corner to let her and Shiloh off.

There was no sign of Fred the Fox and the commune's old Holden, just the old guy in a ute who'd been there yesterday too, sitting on the corner and staring at the school bus as it headed further down the valley.

Fred the Fox was mostly late, Shiloh had told her yesterday afternoon. Either he forgot the time (trying to repair the pump or making a hot-water system out of an old bedstead and black polypipe) or else the car wouldn't start, and Fred had to scrounge a part from one of the wrecks he'd collected before he could get it going again. Shiloh said he'd once almost walked the ten kays up to the commune before Fred came belting down the hill to find him.

Shiloh and Ellen started walking. Ellen waited till they'd turned the first corner then asked, 'Who was that?'

'Who was what?'

'That old guy in the ute.'

'Him? That's just old Mr Picker. He's there every day.' Shiloh picked up a stone and threw it so it landed above their heads in the trunk of a hollow tree.

'Who's he waiting for?'

'His kids.'

'Why weren't they on the bus then? He was waiting there yesterday too, wasn't he?'

At least Fred had arrived on time yesterday. It was bad enough having to stay with your sister in her weird commune while your mum went off to America to finish her MA, thought Ellen, without having to walk home in the heat and dust.

'Look,' said Shiloh, 'there was this accident, see? About ten years ago. The school bus crashed going round the corner. You know the one with the safety rail? Well, that's why there's a safety rail there now: it wasn't there then. And that's why Johnnie Leeham down the pub has only one arm and Mrs Norris at the newsagent's in town has all those scars. Anyway, two kids were killed as well.'

'Mr Picker's kids?'

'Yeah.' Shiloh shaded his eyes and looked up the hill. 'I wish Fred would hurry. This bag weighs a tonne.'

'But that's horrible!'

'Yeah, I suppose,' Shiloh sounded bored. 'Anyway, Mr Picker's wife had died and all he had were these two kids and his farm, and when they died as well, he just went peculiar. Stopped farming and everything or going anywhere, not even down to the pub. And he just sits there every afternoon like he expects the kids to be on the bus.'

'Every afternoon? For ten years?'

'Yep.'

'But how long does he stay there?'

Shiloh shrugged. 'Dunno. He's off his rocker anyway.'

'But how does he live if he doesn't work or get groceries or anything?'

'Big Marge down the valley buys stuff for him and he gets some pension or something. He's pretty old — he had his kids late because of the war and stuff. He was a prisoner of war on the Burma railway, Fred said. Hey, there's Fred. Wonder what went wrong this time.'

'Sorry kids!' Fred flung open the car's front door (the back seat was full of bales of old hay). 'Flat tyre. Good day at school?'

'Nope,' said Shiloh.

'School just indoctrinates you with the outdated fallacies of the bourgeoisie,' said Fred. 'Waste of blooming time if you ask me.' The car swung round, narrowly missing a gum tree, then leapt up the hill. The seat belts were broken, so Ellen hung onto the door handle and hoped.

'Fred?' Ellen's words came out wobbly because of the bumps.

'Yeah?' Fred swerved as a wallaby dashed out of the thorn bushes.

'How long does Mr Picker wait there for his kids?'

'Poor old coot,' said Fred the Fox. 'He usually waits there an hour or so, till he sees the bus head back the other way. Venuswami tried inviting him down to dinner a coupla times when we first came here, but he wasn't having any. Doesn't go anywhere, except down to the bus stop.'

Ellen thought privately that Mr Picker hadn't missed much by not coming to dinner. Wednesday night Venuswami had cooked wholemeal spaghetti that looked like brown worms, with stuff that looked like dog's vomit for dessert, pumpkin and raisin custard, that was it.

But all she said was, 'Poor bloke.'

'Yeah,' said Fred, as the car bumped over the last hole in the road and drew up outside the teepee he shared with Mary and baby Rainbow. 'Here we are then, kids! Pick you up Monday morning.'

Karen's place was down the track from Fred and Mary's teepee. It wasn't really a proper house, thought Ellen, but at least it was better than a teepee with grass matting on its dirt floor, or Fairwind and Venuswami's bamboo dome that leaked in ten different places.

Karen's place had mud-brick walls, with a stone and concrete floor and second-hand windows that did not match each other. It had only one room, with two beds against one wall, a sagging sofa against the other, and an old wood stove that Karen had found on a garbage tip and Fred had hauled home in pieces in the Holden.

You had to go outside to the pit dunny, and even the shower was outside — just a canvas bag and shower head attached to a long length of black polypipe that grew hot in the sun. The wind whistled through the gap under the door, you had to light the gas lanterns to get any light, and bush rats scampered up in the ceiling.

'Karen?'

'I'm out here!'

Ellen dumped her bag inside the faded wooden door and walked over to the vegetable garden. Karen was weeding, a wide hat on her head and her faded orange and red sarong around her. Although she worked Saturdays and Sundays at the milkbar up in town, most of her food came from the garden and the hens that scratched around the young peach trees in the orchard.

Karen had been studying law at uni before she'd decided to buy a share in the commune instead. Land was cheap in the valley — poor steep land like the commune's, anyway — and it was even cheaper shared between three households. It all seemed crazy to Ellen — why spend your days weeding or shovelling hen manure onto peach trees when you could have been clean and comfortable, earning lots of money in an office?

'Good day at school?'

'Okay, I suppose.' Ellen wondered whether to tell Karen about the dinosaur. But she'd probably think she was crazy, just like Shiloh did.

Maybe there was something in this valley that turned you bonkers, she thought grimly, so you called yourself weird names or waited for kids who would never come.

'Hungry? There's some of Fairwind's dried-fig bread on the bench.'

'No thanks.' Ellen thought that maybe one day she'd be hungry enough to eat fig bread, but not today.

'Come and help me pick some salad stuff then. Okay if we eat early?'

'Fine by me.' Actually what she really wanted was a hamburger, two cans of cola, a chocolate Paddle Pop and a TV set — not to mention her own room at home and her own school and her own friends. But there wasn't much she could do about any of it.

Karen looked at her closely, but all she said was, 'We'll have some sweet corn too.'

Dinner wasn't bad — better than worm spaghetti anyway. Even if the lettuce was gritty and there was a grub in the tomatoes, the corn was good and there was plenty of it, with butter from the cow Fairwind kept tethered up behind their dome. And even if Karen didn't have a fridge, the milk was cold from the Coolgardie safe by the back door.

All in all, thought Ellen, it might have been worse.

'Karen?'

'Mmm?' Karen helped herself to more grated carrot and beetroot.

'Are you ever going to have a real house?'

'You think this place isn't real? Like its going to have evaporated one morning when you wake up?'

'You know what I mean — with a proper bathroom and stuff like that.'

'Sure, one day. When I can afford it and have time to build it.'

'But other people have bathrooms straight away.'

'Yeah, sure, and have to take out great loans from the bank and spend all their time in jobs they hate to pay back the bank. No thanks.'

'But…' Ellen shrugged. Like Mum said, what was the use? Karen did what she wanted.

After dinner they read, the gas lights hissing and flickering into the corners of the room and animals scuttling past the windows: the thud of a wallaby, a wombat scratching. Thank goodness the school had a decent library, thought Ellen, or she'd be bored witless.

A scream echoed through the room.

'What was that?'

'A long-fanged vampire about to suck out our blood.'

'Are you serious?'

'Of course not, you dope. It was an owl.'

'Owls say whoo, whoo!'

'Not barking owls. They call them screaming woman birds too.'

'What was wrong with it?'

'Nothing. Just calling another owl.' Karen yawned. 'I'd better get to bed. I've got to be up at the milkbar by seven thirty. Keep reading if you like.'

Ellen shivered. Screaming owls and dinosaurs on rocks. This place was weird. 'No. I'll go to sleep too.'

She wondered, as she drifted off, what noise a dinosaur, like the one she'd seen, made.

⌒

Karen had already left for work when Ellen woke next morning. She considered lighting the stove to heat some water for washing, as Karen had done for her the last two days before school, but she couldn't be bothered. She'd stay dirty for once. There was no one to smell her anyway.

There was homemade bread in the cupboard — lumpy — and home-ground peanut butter — also lumpy — and eggs from the chooks, but she'd have to light the stove to cook them. Ellen felt a sudden longing for cornflakes or Coco Pops ...

A whole day to fill in, all by herself. Well, there were the others on the commune, but they were Karen's age or even older, or babies. Only Shiloh was about her age and he was a twit, making fun of her just because she'd seen a dinosaur ...

It was possible for a dinosaur to live in some out-of-the-way place, wasn't it? Just like that movie. Maybe dinosaurs had been living up in the cliffs above the valley all the time, staying out of humans' way.

Ellen sat up, suddenly determined. She'd find the dinosaur and track it to its lair — that's if dinosaurs had lairs. Maybe they lived in trees or caves. And it wasn't like it was a *big* dinosaur or anything. She supposed there would have been no chance of a big dinosaur staying hidden all this time.

Anyway, she was going to find it. What else was there to do in this dump on a weekend?

⌒

It wasn't easy to work out where the dinosaur rock was. It was back up the valley, she knew that much, but she didn't want to hike all the way down to the road and up the mountain again to see it. There had to be a shorter way across country.

Creeks ran downhill, didn't they? Maybe if she just followed the creek for a while then walked up the ridge, she'd find it.

It was cold down at the creek, despite the growing heat of the day. The water rippled under its sprinkle of casuarina leaves, trickling through the rocks then falling into deeper pools. The pools grew deeper as she went, hopping from rock to rock.

How far had she come? Far enough, probably. Now all she had to do was head up the hill and surely she'd see the rock. It was too big to miss.

It was hot away from the creek. The casuarinas gave way to wattle trees, then fat-trunked gums, then thinner trees as the ground grew stony. An old barbed-wire fence barred the way. She pulled the wire up and clambered through. Surely the rock would be somewhere around here ...

There it was! It looked even larger from here, a great rounded stone like a dinosaur's back, rising high above the valley. But there was no sign of her dinosaur, unless the great rock was its mother, kneeling down. No, she was being stupid like Karen with her vampire story the night before. Ellen clambered up to the rock then scrambled up its side.

The rock looked even more like dinosaur hide now she was close to it, sort of grey and pink and pitted, and warm from the sun. Ellen gazed around. You could see half the valley from up here: Fred and Mary's teepee and the pale snake of the road and an old house half hidden by trees, with a thread of smoke curling from its chimney. Ellen wondered if the house belonged to one of the commune members she hadn't met yet, or whether it was a neighbour.

Her tummy rumbled. Suddenly she wished she'd had some breakfast, even the dry heavy bread or a glass of not-quite-cold milk that was actually really good milk, better than the stuff out of a bottle. Maybe she should have a swim on her way back then...

Something crashed through the bush behind her. Something with heavy feet and a long snaky neck and skin like an old leather sofa, all grey and yellow. Something that gazed at her from beady eyes, with jaws that opened all big and gaping...

'No!' she cried.

It *was* a dinosaur! But why had she ever thought it small? Alright, it wasn't the size of a tyrannosaurus, but it was still as long as she was and much wider. Its legs were thicker than hers too, all shaggy skin and muscle. It lurched through the bush just like the cartoon dinosaurs on TV at home, closer, closer, closer.

The dinosaur stopped. Its beady eyes stared at her. Ellen took three steps back then stopped before she fell off the rock. Why hadn't she thought about what she'd do when she found the dinosaur? What did dinosaurs eat, anyway? Were they dangerous?

The dinosaur's mouth opened in a horrid, reptile grin. She could smell its foul breath.

She had to escape! She had to get away! Whatever dinosaurs ate, it wasn't cornflakes or dried-fig bread...

The dinosaur began to move again.

She scraped her leg shinning down the rock. Her ankle twisted under her as she landed heavily, but it didn't matter: she had to run, she had to escape. She looked behind her. The dinosaur was still there, tramping steadily behind her. She tried to run faster, but her ankle wouldn't let her. She could hear the beast now, getting closer.

Where was the house she'd seen from up on the rock? She had to get to the house! But how could you find a house in all this bush? Suddenly her heart thumped in relief. There it was, a glimpse of yellow through the trees. She hobbled desperately towards it.

Rusty roof and shabby yellow walls, squatting in the middle of unmown grass and shaggy camellia bushes. A run-down hen house hunched on one side, the hens clucking under ancient fruit trees; a scatter of chickens; a tall dunny with peeling paint. The back door was open, though it was too dark to see inside. Ellen limped towards it.

'Help me! Help!'

Through the door and into an old-fashioned laundry with concrete sinks and a copper, up two stairs into a kitchen...

'Help! Please! You have to help me!' she screamed.

The man at the table stood up, blinking. 'What the ...?' He put his reading glasses down on the newspaper on the table and stared at her. 'What do you want?'

It was the man from the bus stop.

'Please, please, a dinosaur is after me!' As soon as she said it, she felt stupid. Who would believe that she was being chased by a dinosaur? But she was, it was out there!

The man didn't laugh. He just stared at her then said, 'Let's see about that, shall we?' and headed for the door. She hobbled after him, down the stairs and out the laundry door again. The dinosaur stood among the shaggy grass, its great head sniffing the wind.

'That's ... that's it!'

The man just nodded. 'Thought it might be.'

'See? It really is a dinosaur!'

'No, it isn't. It's a goanna. It's after my eggs.' He nodded towards the sagging hen house.

'But ... goannas don't grow that big!'

'Yes, they do, if you give 'em enough time. That one's a coupla hundred years old, I reckon. My grandpa used to tell me there were real whoppers in his day. Would stare right into your eyes when you were on horseback.'

'Oh,' said Ellen. Somehow running from a goanna didn't seem as desperate as running from a dinosaur. 'Will ... will it hurt me?'

'Only if you're an egg. Or dead,' he said.

Ellen thought he might smile when he said that, but he didn't.

'Goannas like dead meat,' he explained. 'Rotting. Smellier the better.'

'Eeerk.' Suddenly she began to shake. Goanna or dinosaur, it didn't matter. She'd been scared and she felt stupid and she wasn't sure which was worse, and she was all alone except for a sister she hardly knew in a commune full of weirdos in the hot and scratchy bush and ...

'You'd better come back inside.'

She looked up. The man nodded towards the door. 'Come on. Your leg's bleeding. Better get something on it.'

'It's alright.'

'No, it isn't.' He stomped off without waiting to see if she followed.

It was hot inside the kitchen. The wood stove — a bit like Karen's — breathed out heat. Ellen sat awkwardly at the table while the man foraged in a cupboard and brought out cotton wool and disinfectant.

'This'll sting,' he said.

It did. Ellen sucked in her breath as he covered the scratch with a bandaid. 'Not too bad,' he judged. 'Cuppa tea?'

It seemed rude to say no, even though she didn't like tea. 'Thank you.'

The man turned to the stove and fiddled with the cups and kettle. 'I'm Bill Picker,' he said abruptly.

'My name's Ellen. Ellen Sampson. I ... I'm sorry for running into your house like that. I feel really dumb.'

'Made a bit of a change,' he said. 'Rescuing a lass from a dinosaur.' And for a minute she wondered if he was laughing, but his face didn't move. It looked like it had forgotten how to laugh.

'Do you see the goanna often?'

'Most days. Except in winter. They sleep all winter. Tries to get in the chook house to steal the eggs, but I've made the door too high for it. The chooks can fly in and out but the blighter can't get in. But it keeps trying.'

'Even though it's never made it?'

'Goannas are pretty stupid. Bit like humans, I reckon. Like a biscuit?'

'Please.'

He put a packet on the table. They were chocolate biscuits. Ellen's eyes widened. She hadn't had a chocolate biscuit since she'd been at Karen's. She wondered how many it would be polite to eat. Three? Four? He noticed her expression. 'You hungry?'

'Well — yes. I'm staying down at the commune with my sister while my mum's in America,' she replied.

'Don't they feed you down there?'

'Yes. Weird stuff. Wholemeal spaghetti and bread made out of dried fruit and nuts.'

'Like a coupla chops?'

'Really?'

'Marge Wilson brings them up for me. She and Len kill a sheep once a week.'

'Oh.' Ellen had never eaten a chop from a sheep that someone had killed — well, not someone who knew someone that she knew. But he was already putting them in the fry pan.

The chops were good. So were the chocolate biscuits and the slices of white bread and butter and beetroot from a tin, not the ground. Only the tomatoes and lettuce were fresh, though this tomato didn't have a grub in it.

'How many hens have you got?' asked Ellen, just for something to say.

'Twenty-four. Too many. The silly sods keep sitting on the eggs until the chicks hatch so I get even more of them. See this one?' He held up a large egg. 'Double yolks, I reckon.'

They talked about hens, and that led to lyrebirds — the ones down the creek would scratch your garden worse than chooks, said Mr Picker. And then he told Ellen about the time the creek flooded and the valley was cut off for three weeks, and then about the year the bridge was washed away three times.

It was good to sit in a proper kitchen too, and talk with someone who ... who ... What was it about Mr Picker? wondered Ellen. It wasn't just that he seemed to enjoy talking to her, that he was lonely too and that he really wanted her to be there.

Maybe it was that he seemed to accept her as she was, too. He wasn't waiting for her to exclaim, 'Hey, cool!' about some weird bit of the commune, wasn't looking at her sideways like the other kids at school and wondering if she had green hair because she was staying on a commune, and her sister packed her homemade bread and beansprout sandwiches for lunch. It was just *peaceful* in the kitchen, she decided. Like Mr Picker was a friend, even if he was old enough to be her grandpa.

'I'd better go,' she said at last, reluctantly. 'Karen will be home soon.' She hesitated. 'Can I come again?'

'Next time you're chased by a dinosaur?'

'No, really, I mean ...'

'It's alright, lassie. You can come again. Any time.' He hesitated too. 'It's good to have someone to cook a chop for.'

She was still limping a bit, but her ankle didn't feel too bad now — it'd be okay. He waved to her as she crossed the garden, but he didn't offer to come with her in case she got lost. Ellen supposed he knew the valley so well it didn't occur to him that a stranger might not know it too. And anyway, she remembered, Bill Picker never went anywhere.

Karen was already home when she got back.

'Hi. Been for a swim?'

'Um. Just a walk.' Suddenly she didn't want to tell Karen about the dinosaur — she'd only laugh at her. And she didn't want to tell anyone about Mr Picker either. The commune was Karen's territory, and suddenly Ellen had something of her own too. A friend. A secret friend — Bill Picker.

The weeks went by and things grew better. She made friends at school, and even Shiloh wasn't bad once you got to know him. Shiloh's real love was military magazines. 'But Mum and Fairwind, they hate anything military, you know? I mean it's all peace and anti-war stuff. But I think sometimes you have to fight, maybe not in Vietnam but ...'

No, Shiloh was okay. Even the commune was alright, once you got used to it, especially now Karen was bringing her proper sliced bread back from the milkbar, and proper peanut butter too.

And there was Mr Picker. She managed to get over there every day at the weekends when Karen was working. He showed her how to feed the lamb, an orphan that Mrs Wilson had brought up, or they collected eggs or watched the goanna clamber up onto the hen house and sit there, hissing at the hens and them and the world in general that didn't give a goanna the eggs it deserved.

But mostly they just talked: about the commune and school and Mum studying in America and how Dad had left and got remarried. And sometimes Mr Picker talked too, but only about the long ago: about the old mine up by the waterfall and the cow that swallowed a detonator and blew up in the Taylors' paddock. Or the time they thought the pub was haunted but it was only Ern Swarden's goat that had got stuck in the washing line and had howled to get out. He never spoke of the war, or his children, or his wife, or the accident that had changed his life. He never spoke of that at all.

There were no photos in the house either. Ellen had thought the house would be full of them, like most old people's houses were. In the early days she worried that he might say, 'You must meet my kids one day. You'll like them,' or something else that would give her the creeps. But he didn't.

Sometimes though she thought he paused when they were talking, as though he was listening for children — voices that were never there. But when she said 'Mr Picker,' he always started to talk again. Apart from that the only reminders of his family were the long afternoons he spent waiting at the bus stop, waiting, waiting, on the narrow road that smelt of dust and snake.

Ellen smiled at him now when she passed his ute, and Mr Picker raised a hand in greeting. But he never spoke to her, out there by the bus stop. It was as though those times were his family's and the weekends were hers.

He only mentioned his family once, in all that time.

It was a Saturday afternoon just before Christmas. The cicadas were getting outside the window, the goanna hissing on the chook-house roof. And somehow the subject of the valley Christmas party came up.

'Karen says Santa comes in a ute!' said Ellen happily. 'Every kid in the valley gets a present, even me, and I've only been here three months, and everyone in the valley comes to the party and ... ' Suddenly she stopped. One person wouldn't be coming to the party, and he was staring at her with shadowed eyes.

'Not everyone,' said Mr Picker. 'Some kids will never go to the party again.'

Her voice died away. There was nothing to say — absolutely nothing to say — so she didn't try to say anything, just stammered something and made an excuse and walked out the door.

And all through the party she imagined him there, sitting in his lonely kitchen while the valley partied, listening for the children who would never get another Christmas present, who would never hang another bauble or tinsel on a tree.

Mum sent an enormous parcel from the USA, with 'Not to be opened till Christmas' scrawled on the front. Fred the Fox and Mary decorated the pittosporum tree in front of their teepee with bird seed and chunks of apple and oranges on strings balls for the birds, 'so the birds can have Christmas dinner too'.

Karen and Ellen hauled a big casuarina branch up into the house and stood it up in the corner.

'Karen?'

'Mmm?' Karen pulled another bit of tinsel across the branch.

'Can we have a *real* Christmas dinner?'

Karen grinned. 'One that doesn't disappear when the clock strikes midnight?'

'No tofu or brown rice,' said Ellen firmly. 'A turkey or a roast chicken and baked vegetables and a pudding.'

'Fairwind's going to make his eggplant casserole and ...'

'Karen!'

'Okay. You win. We'll have turkey here for lunch and have dinner with everyone else in the evening and by then you'll be so stuffed you won't have to eat any eggplant.'

'Actually,' said Ellen, 'I almost like eggplant now. If it's cooked with cheese and tomato anyhow. Karen, could we ask Mr Picker to Christmas lunch?'

'Mr Picker?' Karen stared. 'He won't come.'

'I've sort of got to know him,' admitted Ellen. 'I go over there sometimes.'

'Do you? Well, ask him if you like. If you think … I don't know Ellie. Maybe it'll just remind him of what he's lost. Christmas can be difficult for some people.'

Ellen bit her lip. 'Maybe you're right. Maybe.'

⌒

It was a good Christmas. Karen gave her a new pair of sandals that Fairwind had made (Fairwind's name had been Raincloud but he'd changed it last drought when everyone claimed he'd jinxed the rain away) and Ellen gave Karen a big book on how to graft fruit trees. Mum had sent a great warm jacket for her to wear when she went over there later in the holidays and four tie-dyed tee shirts, and a new tape deck that ran on batteries so they could finally have some music.

And Dad had got his act together and sent a cheque that made up for all the presents he'd forgotten and that sent Karen dancing around the room. 'It's enough for a new room, two new rooms if we're careful. A bathroom and a bedroom.'

Then after breakfast Ellen went to see Mr Picker.

⌒

Karen came with her this time, along the path by the creek and up the hill and through the fence. The house looked just the same, its paint peeling and the dribble of smoke from the chimney.

Ellen knocked on the back door. 'Mr Picker? It's me.'

No one answered. Karen looked round the overgrown garden. 'Maybe he's gone for a walk.'

'He never goes for a walk. He's always here.'

'Maybe he's gone to someone else's for Christmas.'

'But he never goes anywhere!' cried Ellen. 'Only down the road to watch the bus go by. Maybe he's hurt, or...' A horrible thought grabbed her. 'Maybe he doesn't realise it's school holidays. Maybe he's waiting for the bus and it never comes and he just waits and waits...' Her voice was rising in a slow wail.

Footsteps sounded down the corridor. 'That you lassie? Thought I heard your voice. I was asleep.' Mr Picker came to the door and peered out. He blinked at Karen. Ellen took a deep breath. 'Mr Picker, this is my sister. Karen, this is Mr Picker.'

'Ellie's told me a lot about you,' said Mr Picker slowly. 'Come in. Come in. I'll put the kettle on.'

'We ... we brought you a Christmas present,' said Ellen nervously. 'And one of Venuswami's wholemeal honey Christmas cakes. It's pretty yuck though,' she admitted as he handed her the packages.

Mr Picker raised an eyebrow. 'Good thing I've got chocolate biscuits then, isn't it?' He touched the parcel a bit dazedly.

'Sorry it's so messy,' apologised Ellen. 'I'm not a good wrapper.'

'It's beautiful,' said Mr Picker quietly. 'Just didn't want to spoil it by opening it too soon, that's all.' He pulled at the sticky tape and ripped the paper away.

It was a plaster dinosaur. Ellen had seen it advertised in a nature magazine at school and written away for it. She watched Mr Picker nervously. It had seemed just the thing when she saw it, but it seemed silly now.

'I thought ... I thought it might remind you ...' she stammered.

'Of the only time in my life I ever rescued someone from a dinosaur? I won't forget that in a hurry. But this'll remind me if I ever start to forget.'

He was almost smiling, thought Ellen. He really did like it she thought, relieved.

Karen frowned. 'Dinosaur? How can you rescue someone from a dinosaur?'

Mr Picker looked from Ellen to Karen and back again. His lips twitched. 'Oh, you can if you're in the right place at the right time.' He paused. 'It just so happens ...' He picked a parcel up off the bench. It wasn't wrapped in Christmas paper, just wrapping paper from a store. 'Merry Christmas,' said Mr Picker.

Ellen unwrapped it slowly. 'It's ... it's a book about dinosaurs!' she said. 'And ... oh, look at this! It's wonderful Mr Picker!'

'It's a dinosaur teapot! Wherever did you find it?' cried Karen.

'I didn't,' said Mr Picker simply. 'Marge Wilson mentioned she'd seen one down the coast on their holidays and so I rang the place up and asked if they'd send me one if I sent the money.'

'It's so ... so silly!' said Karen, delighted. 'Look, you hold its tail and the tea comes out its mouth. I've never seen anything like it.' She glanced at Ellen. 'What is this about dinosaurs, anyway?'

'Oh, nothing,' said Ellen. 'Hey, can we make the tea in it now?'

It was peaceful sitting in the kitchen, pouring cups of tea from the dinosaur's mouth, till finally Karen looked at her watch

'We'd better get back,' she said. 'I left the turkey in the oven. Mr Picker, would you like to have lunch with us? I got a turkey and we made a pudding with Grandma's recipe. It's only next door...' Her voice died away.

Mr Picker was looking out the window, almost as though he still heard children's laughter in the garden. 'No, thank you,' he said quietly, without looking at her. 'I appreciate the thought. But no.'

～

Fred the Fox gave Ellen a belt he'd made himself, even though he said that Christmas was just a patriarchal reworking of ancient pagan customs. And Mary gave her an embroidered patchwork vest, and even Shiloh gave her a present — a packet of bath salts. She'd have to use them in the old bath up on bricks out the back that Karen filled with buckets from the stove, but it was still nice of him, and she'd given him a copy of *Guns and Hunters* magazine in return.

It was a good Christmas. But all through the laughter and the presents she remembered the old man and his silent voices up on the hill.

～

New Year's Eve meant a party at the community hall up the valley; New Year's Day there were sports for the kids and a barbecue. (Venuswami brought corn cobs and vegie kebabs to grill for the vegetarians, but Ellen still managed to scrounge a steak and three fat sausages. Karen had given in and was buying meat and even Coco Pops nowadays.)

A few days later Karen borrowed the car again from Fred the Fox and drove Ellen up to Sydney to catch the plane for San Francisco to stay with Mum.

The flight was terrifying and exciting and boring all at once. It was wonderful to see Mum and ride the cable car and do a hundred different things. Ellen sent postcards to everyone, including Shiloh and Mr Picker. And suddenly January was over and so was her holiday, and there was Karen waiting at the airport and balloons on the rusty old gate at the commune and suddenly, as they bumped along the track, it felt like home, not weird at all.

So much had happened in a month. The teepee had a new greenhouse, all glass and green plants, and Shiloh had grown another two inches and, most surprising of all, Karen's house had three new rooms. Ellen flew through the house and down the new passage and opened the doors — two tiny bedrooms and ... 'A bathroom! A real bathroom!'

'Yep. Won't even vanish if you shut your eyes. Just don't use the toilet or you'll get a nasty surprise. Fred hasn't connected it yet.'

'Where does all the yuck go?'

'Down into a septic tank down the hill. I'll show you later.' Karen laughed in delight. 'We all worked like mad to get your room ready for when you got back. Venuswami painted those flowers round the ceiling, and Fairwind made the rug, and Mary made the patchwork quilt and ...'

Karen sat on the bed while Ellen unpacked slowly in her new room. The walls were mud brick like the rest of the house, and the floor was flat river stones set in concrete. Ellen blinked at one of them. 'Hey, that rock sort of glows.'

Karen grinned. 'Yep,' she said with a mock-American accent. 'There's gold in that there rock, pardner.'

'You're joking? Aren't you?'

'Nope. That's gold alright. When we were collecting all the paving stones Venuswami found that one with a bit of gold in it. She thought it'd be nice by your bed. You know, every morning you're stepping out on gold.'

'You mean it's real?'

'Sure. There's gold all through the valley. Didn't you know?'

Ellen shook her head. 'Mr Picker said there were old mines. I didn't know there was still gold here. Isn't that worth thousands of dollars?'

Karen laughed. 'That little bit of gold? No way. About ten dollars, maybe. But it's pretty.'

'Sure is.'

'You sound like a Yank. How's Mum enjoying it over there?'

Ellen hesitated. 'She's been offered a job. It all depends on work permits, but I think she's going to take it. She said I could go to school over there.'

Karen met her eyes. 'Want to?'

Ellen shrugged, unwilling to commit herself.

'You know, said Karen lightly, 'you could always just stay here.'

'For good?'

'Why not? Build yourself your own house when you're sick of staying with me. But not for a few years yet, not after all the work finishing your bedroom.'

'That might be fun,' said Ellen.

'No need to decide yet, anyway. By the way, I've enrolled in law again.'

Ellen looked up in alarm.

'So you'll be going away?'

'No way. I'm an external student. And I get to keep all the credits for the stuff I've done already.'

'So when will you be a lawyer?'

'Two years. Maybe.' Karen stood up. 'Come on, come and have a swim. I want to wash all the Sydney dirt off.'

It was wonderful to lie back in the creek again, to feel the cold water wash over her, to see the casuarina trees high against the blue and watch the kookaburras swoop down to catch the tiny fish in the pools.

It was great to see everyone too and catch up on what had happened while she was away. Venuswami had got a copy of the Moosewood cookbook and had baked her a welcome-home banana cake that actually tasted like cake should taste, and oat and carob muffins that were pretty good too.

The peaches were ripe on the young trees and when she walked over the hill she found that Mr Picker had pinned her postcards up on his kitchen wall, 'where I can see them every time I have a cuppa tea.' He hesitated. 'I missed you, lassie.'

'I missed you too,' admitted Ellen, and it was true.

February brought school and the school play, where Ellen got the lead part. The swimming carnival was in February too and Shiloh won the breast stroke. Ellen won the CWA prize for her project on Tibet.

Floribelle had a calf in March, and Ellen and Shiloh got to watch it being born, while eating Venuswami's date and walnut bread, and carrot and tofu pie with peanut sauce. A year ago it would have seemed weird to have a picnic while a calf was being born, thought Ellen. But now it was the most fascinating thing she'd ever seen. Fred and Mary bought a pair of goats and kept them tethered in the orchard till they ate half the trees, then they fenced off a paddock for them instead. Mary made goats' milk cheese for a while then gave it up, and they all just drank the milk instead.

April brought blue skies and soft clear sunlight, falling leaves and ripe brown pears in Mr Picker's garden. April also brought the gold miners, and change.

⌒

The first mention was in the local paper. Ellen came home from school to find Karen holding it dazedly in front of her.

'What's wrong?'

Karen passed the paper over. 'It's a mining company. They want to look for gold, here in the valley.'

'Can they do that? Without asking?'

'Not near houses and orchards and things. But if people give them permission, yes, of course they can.'

'Do you think people would?'

Karen bit her lip. 'I don't know. Maybe. Yes, very likely. Mines mean jobs and more money for the pub and people who sell petrol and stuff up in town. And they'll probably offer people money too, just to let them on their land. Oh, Ellie, it's so horrible! After all we've done here.'

'But … but would it be so very bad? I mean if it was just a little mine?'

'Mines use water, lots of water, and the gold is all around the creek, that's where the gold mining was years ago. I suppose modern methods mean they can get more of it out — yes, it would be bad. It'd mean pollution and heavy metals in the water and mud and noise and trucks. We'd lose everything that makes this place so special!'

'Can't we just tell everyone how bad it'd be?'

'Maybe. It's all such a shock. There's a meeting down at the hall tonight. The mining guy is going to speak — tell everyone how great the mine would be for the local economy, I bet. Maybe we've got a chance to stop it.'

She sighed. 'I'd better go up to Fred and Mary's before dinner. We have to talk about this. We have to work out what to say at the meeting. Oh, it's all so awful.'

❧

Ellen cooked dinner — she knew how to manage the wood stove now. Karen hurried back into the hut just as she was mashing the potatoes. Karen's face was tense. 'We'll all to go to the hall together,' she told Ellen. 'We have to convince people somehow. We have to!'

Dinner was solemn. It seemed impossible to Ellen that things could change so suddenly — that one day the valley could be paradise, and the next dug up and mined.

They walked up to Fred and Mary's by torchlight. The days were shorter now. The air smelt of autumn and fallen peach leaves and cold rocks from the creek.

Fred was wearing his clean overalls and Mary her best long Indian dress with embroidery on the bottom, and bangles on her ankles. They all crammed into the Holden.

'Have you brought...' began Venuswami, then stopped as Fred turned the key in the ignition and nothing happened.

Fred tried again.

Silence.

Fred swore and slammed out of the car and opened the bonnet. He fiddled for a moment. 'Try it again!' he yelled.

Mary edged over and turned the key. Still nothing.

'What's wrong?' she called.

'No idea.' Fred swore again. 'I need flaming daylight, not torchlight.'

'How long will it take to fix it?' asked Karen anxiously.

'How do I know? An hour? A week? Look, just hold the torch for me and I'll try.'

They got out of the car and crowded round, then moved back when Fred swore at them.

'Maybe we should start walking,' suggested Ellen quietly.

'It's twelve kilometres down to the hall!' protested Karen. 'It'll take us at least an hour and a half. The meeting starts in ten minutes!'

'Maybe if we ran down to the main road we could hitch a ride.'

'We could try. But I bet everyone's there already. There's only the Wilsons and the Greens down past our place anyway. Why did it have to happen now?' cried Karen. 'Any other day than this! If only we had another car!'

Ellen touched her arm. 'Karen?'

'What?'

'I know where there's another car. Mr Picker's.'

'But he never goes anywhere! There's no point even asking him!'

'I can try! Look, if Fred gets the car going, you can pick me up at his place. But I've got to try!'

'Ellen, no!'

It was too late. Ellen — and their torch — disappeared down the track.

⌒

The night closed around her. Possums scuffled in the trees. A wallaby looked up from drinking at the creek, considered, then bent down to the water again. Ellen was no threat, and he was thirsty.

Ellen ran along the creek. It looked different in darkness. The way seemed longer, rougher. Yes, here was the turn — up the hill and through the fence and across the tangled garden. The big camellia tree was just bursting into flower.

'Mr Picker! Mr Picker!'

'What is it, lassie? What's wrong?' His glance was white in the darkness. 'Has there been an accident?'

'No, no, nothing like that. Please, it's urgent — Fred's car won't start. Can you drive us down to the hall?'

Mr Picker frowned as though he didn't understand. 'The hall? But why?'

'The miners — they're going to ask permission from everyone to prospect on their places. And we've got to stop them. It will be terrible if there's a mine here. Please, Mr Picker, please.'

'But ...' He hesitated then shook his head. 'No. I'm sorry, lassie. But no.'

'Please! It's ... it's the most important thing in all my life.' And suddenly she realised that it was, that she loved this valley; loved the hills and the way the moonlight seemed to collect in the gullies and trickle down through the trees. Somehow the valley had come to mean more to her than anything else she'd known.

'Lots of things are important, girl.' He stopped. For a moment he seemed to listen to his lost voice again, then he looked at her face.

'Alright,' he said abruptly. 'Stay here while I get my keys.'

Fred was still under the bonnet of the car when the ute pulled up. Karen ran towards them. 'Ellen, how did you...?' she stopped and said hesitantly, 'Mr Picker, I don't know how to thank...'

'Just get in!' urged Ellen. 'We're late!'

Karen squeezed into the seat next to Ellen, with Rainbow on her knee, and the others piled into the back of the ute.

The community hall was down the road from the pub, with the tennis courts behind it and a cluster of houses all around. Light spilled out of the door and cars lined the road, utes mostly, with the odd green truck or Holden.

The hall was full already. Fifty, no sixty people, thought Ellen, as they found seats at the back. No one seemed to notice them. Most of the men held schooners of beer from the pub down the road; a few of the women were knitting or feeding babies. A tall man in a grey suit stood at the front. It looked like he had been speaking for a while.

'... and just in conclusion,' he said, smiling earnestly at the audience, 'I'd like to say that every one of you here is possibly sitting on a fabulous resource. If you give us permission to prospect here, and we find the gold I think we're going to find, some of you are going to make a fortune here in the valley. We'll pay you to mine on your properties. And that money will stay in the valley. But that's not all. A mine here will mean jobs.'

'So now,' the man in the suit nodded at a man in the front row, 'this is Alan Jordan from our company's legal department. He's going to read out the affected landowners' names one by one, and I'd like you to call out if you give us permission to prospect here or not.'

'I know you hear stories of mines where things go wrong,' he added, 'but we're not like that. We're a big company, not some little fly-by-night. We'll be here for the long haul. Now, Alan ...'

'We're too late!' whispered Ellen.

Karen nodded, her eyes bleak.

'But they can't agree! They can't!' hissed Venuswami.

Mr Jordan took out his fountain pen. 'If you'd just answer when I call your names ...' he said. 'William Picker.'

'Not here,' said someone. 'You'll have to go up to his place if you want to talk to Bill.'

'I'm here.'

Someone gasped. Heads turned round towards them.

Mr Picker stood up stiffly. 'There's just one thing I want to say,' he said. 'If my kids had lived, I'd want to see them out in the sunlight where they belonged, not buried in some mine.' He paused, then said abruptly, 'That's all I want to say. Oh, and the answer's no.'

People were still muttering in front. But the lawyer didn't seem to realise anything momentous had happened. He ran his pen down the list again. 'Keith McKenzie?'

An old man with thin lips stood up. 'No.'

Mr Jordan blinked. 'You don't give permission either?'

'No.' He sat down again.

'Henry Jacobs.'

Another man stood. 'No.'

'Mrs Hilda Bowker.'

A woman in the back row put down her knitting — it was a striped tea cosy — and stood up.

'No.'

'Samuel Taylor.'

'No.'

'Richard Ferris.'

'Nope.'

'I don't believe it,' whispered Venuswami.

'Helen MacDonald.'

'No.'

'Walter ...' The first man shook his head at Mr Jordan. He stood up again and looked around the meeting. 'I think you're all making a big mistake,' he said shortly, 'but that's your decision.' He gathered up his briefcase and walked out of the hall. Mr Jordan followed him. Neither looked back.

Someone laughed. A few whispers ran around the room. The Chairman out the front with the gavel banged it on the table. 'Well, if no one's got anything more to add, I now declare this meeting over. Ern, get me a refill, will you?'

Ellen sat stunned. 'They don't want the mine either,' she whispered.

Karen bit her lip and looked at Mr Picker. 'You convinced them,' she said. 'What you said about your kids.'

Mr Picker shook his head. 'No, lassie,' he said, 'they none of them would have wanted it. Anyone who's lived their life in this valley knows what the mining did to it. There was never any danger of someone saying yes.' He looked like he was going to say something more, then shook his head just as someone clapped him on the shoulder. 'Well, Bill you old ...' Suddenly he was lost in a crowd of friends.

Fred the Fox shouldered his way towards them, carrying a tray. He must have been over to the pub, Ellen realised. He handed her a cola and a packet of chips.

Ellen stared at the cola. 'You said that cola is an oligarchical capitalist conspiracy to subvert Australia's national cultural identity.'

'Did I?' asked Fred. 'What the heck. This is a celebration. Let me know when you want a refill.'

Ellen sat and listened to the talk around her — Venuswami discussing moon planting, and Fred the Fox offering to fix someone's ute in return for a day's use of a tractor, and Shiloh asking Mr MacDonald how you went about getting a shooter's licence, and Karen telling Mrs Swanson how she could make her own will without paying a solicitor in town. The talk flowed around her, and suddenly the people from the commune sounded like all the others in the hall. I belong here, thought Ellen sleepily. We all belong.

'Time to go home?' It was Mr Picker. 'You've got school tomorrow.'

'Yes,' said Ellen gratefully. 'Yes, please.'

She sat in the back on the way home and felt the wind in her hair and Karen's arm warm around her. The moon was just rising over the ridges, spilling its gold down the slopes.

Ellen lingered as they all piled out at the teepee. She waited till the others had wandered down the track and Fred and Mary had pulled the teepee flap closed. Karen caught her eye and stepped away from the ute, as Ellen peered in the window towards Mr Picker.

'Mr Picker ...' she began. And suddenly Ellen found the words she'd wanted to say ever since Shiloh had told her Mr Picker's story.

'Mr Picker, I'm sorry about your kids. I'm really sorry.'

Mr Picker stared at her, his face like a dried-up apple in the dark. Then he smiled. It wasn't much of a smile; his wrinkles got in the way.

'I reckon I've got my kids right here,' he said. 'You and Shiloh want a lift down to the bus tomorrow? Pick you up in the afternoon too, if you like.'

Ellen had been half hoping they'd get a day off school, with the car out of commission, but she said 'Yes, please' anyway.

The smile widened, just a bit. 'See you tomorrow then,' said Mr Picker, as he gunned the motor. The ute bumped down the road through the dusty moonlight.

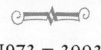

## 1972 – 2002

Ironically it was the new settlers in the valley, who cared so deeply about the land, who may have done more damage than even the miners, by bringing in goats that escaped from their tethers and became feral pests, clambering up the rocky hills and pulling small trees and shrubs out by their roots.

There are thousands of wild goats now in the valley. The gullies that once sheltered maidenhair ferns and tree ferns are barren and eroding; the floods are frothy with mud again. The valley recovered from every other change, but goats have brought desert to too many other parts of the world. If no one can find a way to control them in the wild and rocky cliffs, one day the valley may be desert too.

And there are other pests: wild cats and foxes that kill the lyrebirds, so every winter there are fewer songs from the gullies. The dingoes have long ago been killed, but there are wild dogs now that kill the stock and wallabies and wombats, and some farmers still shoot the parrots, bower birds and fruit bats that eat their fruit (or poison enormous flocks of them).

For the first time in eighty million years there is no river running through the valley. Up on the tablelands, hobby farmers and retirees plant big gardens and sink bores to water them, so very little flows into the valley and it's soon gone, sucked up by the pumps that water the orchards. The only time the river flows now is after a flood or in the winter, when a thin green trickle washes over the sand.

More people have come to the valley. For the first time people live in the valley who haven't walked its hills or ridden them on horseback. They are absentee landlords who come down to the valley for holidays or for weekends, or just dream of retiring to the bush.

Often they spend so little time in the valley that they don't realise its problems. They don't help control the feral animals like goats, pigs, cats and foxes, they don't join the bush fire brigade and help fight fires. Small blocks of land that haven't been used since the mining days have been sold again and houses built on them, and larger farms have been divided into forty hectare blocks.

Most people in the valley no longer farm now, though peach orchards still line the valley. (There isn't enough water to grow many vegetable crops any more, and besides, the prices are lower these days. Most of the vegetables that people buy now are grown more cheaply thousands of kilometres away or even in other countries, in places where the crops can be irrigated.)

Some people in the valley are retired. Some telecommute: use their computers and phone lines to do work for city firms, even though they are hundreds or thousands of kilometres away. Others are unemployed and live here because the houses are cheap to rent. Some work in town, once a day's ride away or three days droving the cattle, but now a twenty-minute drive.

Have I made it sound as though the valley is a dismal place, the hills eroding, the river dead with sand?

It's not. It is the most lovely place I know. The ridges rise just as they did forty thousand years ago when the first humans wandered up the river. National Park surrounds two sides of the valley now, and even if there is no money to keep weeds or feral animals from breeding in the park, the land is safe from clearing and from mining.

Even the old mullock heaps and sandy creek flats turned over by the dredges are being restored — turned into orchards, with drip irrigation and mown lucerne between the trees so they use less water. Trees have been planted in eroded gullies. The valley's inhabitants work together (mostly, anyhow) to make the best use of the valley's limited water and to fight bushfires. There is still a Christmas party for the valley children, as there has been for a hundred and fifty years, though Santa today comes in a dusty ute, not a horse and cart.

And if you come to the valley you can still pan for gold in the creek and find tiny flecks that glitter in the sand. The eagles still soar on the thermals as the hot air rises from the valley.

Sometimes it is as though the valley is a world apart.

The land where I live has been cleared for farming, mining and logging, for fence posts and firewood for the dredges, but in the thirty years I've been here the bush had grown back, and if I decided to live without supermarkets and vegie gardens, the bush would still feed me and my family.

As I look out the window of my study I can see literally hundreds of different types of food — probably more than in a supermarket, though you have to know how to find and harvest and prepare them. Sandpaper figs, seeds from the sharp-edged 'blady grass', sedges, tree ferns with their cabbage-like centres, wild raspberries, native cherries, plantain—long purple-orange kangaroo berries, and climbing wombat berries that have a thick tasty root as well as their round orange fruit.

Next spring there'll be grass orchids under those trees — they're a bit like sweet potato when you bake them. There is watercress in the creek (introduced from Europe), and wild spinach, mistletoe berries, backhousia trees (I use their fragrant leaves as seasoning in cooking), wattle trees for gum and galls, and the hymenanthera thorn bushes with their oily, nutritious seeds and sweet blossom.

There are kurrajong trees too. Kurrajong fruit is edible and sometimes very good — like most 'wild' trees the quality of fruit varies a lot. The young roots are also good baked in the ashes like potatoes, but old ones can be bitter and fibrous. Be careful how many kurrajong roots you dig up — if you dig too many you'll kill the tree.

As it matures, kurrajong fruit turns into long pods of brown seeds. These seeds are very good to eat, but you have to know how to gather them and cook them, as the hairs around the inside of the seed pods are poisonous and very irritating. It's best to just eat the fruit and leave the seeds alone.

If I was very hungry, I could catch yabbies or look for freshwater mussels or if I was starving I could even catch frogs. (But only if I were starving — frogs are dying out and need to be protected.) There are wallabies and kangaroos, sweet lerps on the eucalyptus leaves, fat moths sometimes (they don't taste too bad roasted on the fire), and even grasshoppers taste good, as long as they haven't been feeding on poisonous plants that will poison you too. I could climb that tree with the scratches and the possum dung below, and stick my hand in the big hole and maybe capture dinner (or maybe get bitten by the black snake that might live there instead ... but then snakes make good tucker too if you avoid their poison glands).

Nearly two hundred years after white settlers came to this valley, it is still a generous place to live, and as well as the 'bush tucker' there are new foods too. There are peach orchards down the valley, paddocks of pumpkins, bee hives and cattle, and gardens and orchards like ours. (We have almost three hundred sorts of fruit growing here, and dozens of vegetables and hundreds of herbs.)

This valley has been one of the best spots for good tucker for many animals, including humans, for hundreds of thousands of years. Even in the twenty-first century, it's still a place where you can pick your fruit as the lyrebirds sing, and munch it on the banks of the creek.

## A TRUE STORY

This is the last of the stories about the valley and its gold, and it's a true story.

The first gold I found was in a boulder, big and round and grey and pink. I was collecting rocks to build our stone house and this one rolled off the tray of the green truck and split in two, and there in the middle was an almost perfect nugget of gold.

No, I didn't shriek, 'Gold! Gold! I'm rich!' It was a pretty small lump of gold and, anyway, I didn't know who to sell it to. So when I put all the other rocks into their piles — flat-sided ones for the front of the walls and brick-like ones for corners — I put the rock containing the gold to one side.

Well, it was hot the next day, and a mob of friends came down to swim in the creek. They helped us build the next bit of house wall before we all plunged into the swimming hole. There was lots of laughter and people who'd never built a stone wall before getting covered in dust and concrete. It wasn't till we wandered back from the creek to pick plums and lettuce for lunch that I realised my gold rock had gone. Someone had built it into the walls of the house.

No, I didn't start tearing the walls down. It's not easy to tear down stone walls and, anyway, I wanted a house to live in more than I wanted a small gold nugget. The gold — or the money it might have been turned into — just didn't seem important.

But I promised you a story …

⌒

It was last Christmas. Christmas morning was clear and bright, but during the afternoon smoke slowly sifted through the trees. My husband Bryan was called up to the Fire Control to man the bushfire radio in mid-afternoon, and that was pretty much the last I saw of him for the next three weeks, except for his exhausted face as he dropped into bed.

Most of the fires had been lit by humans, as almost all bad bushfires are. The one near us came from either a 'control burn', or two lightning strikes (there's a fair bit of argument about which it was), but either way, the fire was left to burn for weeks in the National Park, until hot winds blew burning leaves and bark so far that fires sparked up twenty kilometres from the main fire front.

People came from Queensland and Victoria to help us fight it, but it had been left too long. It was in wild country now. We could only wait and hope the firebreaks would hold it, but every day the smoke grew thicker, and at night when I walked up to the ridges, I could see the rim of red blazing up into the sky.

I packed our most valuable things in case we had to get out in a hurry: the books I love most and photos and contracts and computer discs with stories I was working on and a bag of clothes too. The things that are closest to my heart I couldn't pack into a suitcase: family and friends and wombats and the garden and the bush around me.

The twenty-third day was the worst. The smoke was so dense I found it hard to breathe. You couldn't see the sky or even the end of the garden. The world was white and quiet. All at once a bird arrowed across the garden and fell by the side of our garden pond. I ran out to see what it was. I had never seen a bird like this before — about the size of a rosella, but totally grey. It was a rosella. It had been burnt in the fire — had flown through it, perhaps. But as I watched, it recovered and began to drink.

So I sat on the garden seat next to it while it gasped and drank some more, and I looked out at the garden I couldn't see and the valley I couldn't see either, and ...

No, I don't believe in ghosts. I just hadn't had enough sleep, that was all. But I began to imagine that out there in the whiteness the valley had changed. There was no valley, just the plains of the Gondwanaland of so many million years ago; somewhere in the smoke dinosaurs roamed, or giant wombats, marsupial lions and flat-faced giant kangaroos.

I had been terrified the valley would be destroyed as the fire swept up it. But the valley has been destroyed many times. The treed hills, I know, were bare just thirty years ago when I came here, cleared for grazing and trodden hard by cattle who ate the seedling trees and whose heavy feet trampled the soil, so the first ten years I was here, the hills kept slumping into orange clay landslides.

A hundred years ago half the ridges had been cleared for wood for the gold dredges, and the valley had been mounds of sand and rock. Fifty years before that forty thousand people lived in this valley, and fifty years before that — and for forty thousand years perhaps — hundreds of people gathered in this valley every few years, to feast and to hold ceremonies while the land slowly changed from warm to cold, to dry or wet and back again.

And I realised that while the present matters so much to us, it's just a blink in time. Things pass, even bushfires. Land recovers, even if it isn't in your lifetime; even if it will never be what it was before.

I sat there in the garden, and even when the first drops of water fell on my face I didn't realise what they were; it had been so long since it had rained, and anyway, I was dreaming of forty thousand years ago.

Then ten seconds later the smoke was washed away as the rain fell in sheets of grey, and twenty minutes after that the ground began to shake as the flood shuddered down the creek bringing more gold too, I suppose, though I haven't bothered sifting through the gravel yet to see.

There has always been gold in this valley for everyone who comes here. But there are different kinds of gold, and mine will never be the sort you paddle for in the creek.

Ps. I would like to say that one day when I was really broke I saw the gold nugget gleam at me from the wall, and I sold it and saved the farm … or that I watch it shine at me as I write and it inspires me, but nothing like that has ever happened. The reality isn't as romantic, but it's a lot more satisfying.

And that is the end of the story of the valley and its gold. But of course it's not really the end. The gold is still there, glittering flakes among the sand, and in ten years or a hundred, humans may hunt for it again, for no real reason except that it is beautiful, and so we have valued it almost as long as we have been human. (Pumpkins are more useful than gold, but no one has ever got rich finding pumpkins.)

And of course there is no real ending to any of the other stories either. The diprotodons may have died, but their cousins the wombats still live in the valley. The descendants of Mirrigan, Mary Anne, Sam, Florrie, and Ellen and her yowie still live here too, and so do the hippies, though if you see them now, they look no different from any other farmer in the valley.

And the valley is here too of course, and it's still changing, as it's changed throughout its history.

I've lived in the valley for most of my life. My ancestors lived here too, though I don't think any of them mined for gold. Maybe our family is immune to gold fever. But Peter Ffrench, my great something grandfather, made his fortune (not a very big one — just enough to buy a farm) driving the bullock drays that brought the miners their supplies, and my great grandparents on my mother's side taught the miners' children in the one-roomed school over the hills from where I live now.

Every step I take walks on history. A mining race runs through our property. Built by the Chinese miners, it was an extraordinary piece of engineering that carried water over ten kilometres to wash the gold out of dry seams. It was used again last century to bring water to market gardens.

As I look out my study window, I can see mullock heaps of discarded rocks — Bryan has turned them into gardens and used them to make the rough stone fireplace by the creek where we have barbecues in autumn, and where I used to cook in my earliest days here when, like the miners, I too lived in a tent. (And then in a shed, a bit like the settlers' shacks, with candlelight and no hot water unless I boiled the billy on the fire.)

When I dug down next to the fireplace, I found a lower fireplace and one below that and another below that too. I have a feeling that there has been a fire in that lovely sheltered spot by the creek for many thousands of years, and as each flood washes sand over one fireplace, another is built on top.

Like everyone who has lived in the valley — the diprotodons or, the ancient humans of forty thousand years ago, or the gold miners, or the cattle farmers and the orchardists — I have changed my part of the valley too.

I've let eroding hills go back to trees, so it's hard to see that they were ever cleared. I've planted fruit trees, and some have gone wild as the birds have carried avocado seeds and tamarillos into the wet gullies. If humans disappeared tomorrow, the fruit I planted would keep on growing here.

More than a hundred types of birds feast on the fruit and flowers that we grow here, so even though large parts of the bush around us have been cleared, more birds and animals can survive. And the valley has changed me too, as it changes anyone who lives here who looks out beyond their TV set and their front door.

To say I love the valley is an understatement. I've walked its hills, studied its plants, animals and insects for thirty years, watched for the wonga blossom in spring, and know which wombat holes are ancient and which were dug last year.

I would hate to live in a city, where the only things that influenced me were human: TV, books, computers, other humans' talk; where every track I travelled on and every landscape was made by human hands and human minds.

Here I'm a part — a very small part — of an enormous complexity. It's fascinating. It's ever-changing. And above all things I wish that I could know the next four billion years of its history, as I know at least the outline of its past.

This valley was shaped by my ancestors. Wherever you live, the earth beneath your feet is made of the bones of the ancestors of all of us, and from the plants they grew and the trees they harvested. The way they chose to live has shaped the way we live now.

And the valleys of the future? They will be made by us — by you, by me, and by our children.

# Other books by Jackie French

## Fiction

The Roo that Won the Melbourne Cup

Rain Stones

Walking the Boundaries

The Boy Who Had Wings

Somewhere Around the Corner

Annie's Pouch • Alien Games

The Secret Beach

Mermaids • Mind's Eye

A Wombat Named Bosco

Summerland • Beyond the Boundaries

The Warrior — the Story of a Wombat

The Book of Unicorns • Dancing with Ben Hall

Soldier on the Hill • Daughter of the Regiment

Stories to Eat with a Banana • Tajore Arkle

Hitler's Daughter • In the Blood

Missing You, Love Sara

Stories to Eat with a Watermelon

Lady Dance

Stories to Eat with a Blood Plum

How the Finnegans Saved the Ship

Dark Wind Blowing

A Story to Eat with a Mandarin

Ride the Wild Wind

Blood Moon • The White Ship

Phredde and the Leopard-skin Librarian

Diary of a Wombat

*Non-fiction*
How the Aliens from Alpha Centauri Invaded My
Maths Class and Turned Me
Into a Writer …
How to Guzzle Your Garden
Book of Challenges
Stamp Stomp Womp & Other Interesting Ways to
Kill Pests
Seasons of Content
The Best of Jackie French
Earthly Delights
The Fascinating History of Your Lunch
The Secret Life of Santa Claus

*Coming soon*
Big Burps, Bare Bums and Other Bad-mannered Blunders
— 365 Tips on how to Behave Nicely
My Mum the Pirate
My Dog the Dinosaur
Phredde and the Purple Pyramid

---

## *Visit Jackie's website*
**www.jackiefrench.com**
**or**
**www.harpercollins.com.au/jackiefrench**
**for copies of her monthly newsletter**

Some other great historical titles from
HarperCollins*Publishers*

## HITLER'S DAUGHTER
### by Jackie French

The bombs were falling, the smoke was rising from the concentration camps, but all Hitler's daughters knew was the world lessons with Fraulein Gelber, and the hedgehogs she rescued from the cold.

Was it just a story? Did Hitler's daughter really exist? If you were Hitler's daughter, would it all be your fault too? Was it all so long ago it didn't matter ... or did Mark have to face the same question ...

ISBN: 0-207-19801-2

## HOW THE FINNEGANS SAVED THE SHIP
### by Jackie French

Mrs Finnegan and her seven children have to leave Ireland and join Mr Finnegan in Australia. They board a ship which doesn't look as if it can move from the harbour and the Finnegans are nervous ... it is the year after the *Titanic* sank after all.

Mrs Finnegan is busy during the journey saving the ship from whales and other possible disasters. But as they sail around the tip of Africa, an in iceberg looms out of the ocean.

Can the Finnegans save the ship this time?

Inspired by actual events, *How the Finnegans Saved the Ship* tells the story of one Irish family's migration to Australia in 1913. The Finnegan children are confident and prepared to sail around the world, but there are some adventures that could shake anyone's faith.

ISBN: 0-207-19749-0

## LADY DANCE
### by Jackie French

'*Have you ever know what it is like to wait to die? To sit with the smell of death and wait for it to come to you?*'

*I did. I watched my family sicken. I'd cleaned up their vomit and mopped their brows, but they all died anyway. Most people died quickly from the plague.*

*Then I heard music, and a voice: 'Dance!' she cried. 'If you dance then death can't catch you.'*

*Who was lady dance, I wondered, as we danced and sang through empty villages. Was she an angel sent to protect us, as Old Sure said?*

*When Lady Dance sang I saw a new larger world; a world filled with hope and happiness, knights riding to Jerusalem and kings fighting for kingdoms — and I knew I had to find the world for myself.*

Set in the Middle Ages when the bubonic plague was at its height, *Lady Dance* is an extraordinary story of love and the meeting of hearts and minds in the most unlikely circumstances.

ISBN: 0-207-19747-4

## THE WHITE WHIP
### by Jackie French

Michel was happy living with his family on a remote island off the coast of France. But one day disaster strikes the island, and Michel and the other children are forced to flee from Catherine de Medici's soldiers on the White Ship and look for a new land to call home.

Finally Michel's dream has come true — but at what cost? And, what's more, something strange is happening to the White Ship: the ship never weighs anchor, no one grows any older, and they never sight land. What's happening to them? And why is Michel haunted by bizarre dreams of an island in a distant southern land and a girl called Rachel?

*The White Ship* is a story of religious persecution, friendship, and an idealism that stretches over four hundred years; but most of all, it's a story about the search for safe harbour and a place to call home.

ISBN: 0-207-1978-9